A TOBY PETERS MYSTERY

MURDER ON THE
YELLOW BRICK ROAD

STUART M. KAMINSKY received the 1990 Edgar Allen Poe Award for Best Mystery Novel, as well as France's *Grand Prix de Roman d'Aventures* in 1991. His love of the movies—and long academic career as a professor of film history—led him to create the popular and critically acclaimed Toby Peters mystery series. He lives in Florida.

"Kaminsky has the pro's knack of combining quirky people, succinct descriptions, an eye for detail, and dark humor to produce entertainment at its best."

Chicago Sun-Times

"A gifted writer who has created a host of entertaining characters and good stories, largely through humor and a quiet sense of humanity."

Twentieth Century Crime & Mystery Writers

"Toby Peters fans always look forward to the next installment in this unique series . . . full of high good humor and completely credible . . . Kaminsky is well steeped in the legend and lore of wartime L.A., and reading these mysteries is like immersing yourself in the world of *film noir* . . . Consistently well written and enjoyable, the Toby Peters series is for any mystery buff who is also an old film buff."

Mostly Murder

AVAILABLE NOW

AMOS WALKER MYSTERIES
Motor City Blue
by Loren D. Estleman

Angel Eyes
by Loren D. Estleman

The Midnight Man
by Loren D. Estleman

MOSES WINE MYSTERIES
The Big Fix
by Roger L. Simon

The Lost Coast
by Roger L. Simon

SHERLOCK HOLMES MYSTERIES
Revenge of the Hound
by Michael Hardwick

PHILIP MARLOWE MYSTERIES
Raymond Chandler's Philip Marlowe
Anthology; Byron Preiss, Editor

COMING SOON

Sherlock Holmes vs. Dracula
by Loren D. Estleman

Wild Turkey
A Moses Wine Mystery
by Roger L. Simon

The Devil Met a Lady
A Toby Peters Mystery
by Stuart M. Kaminsky

Laura
by Vera Caspary

The Vertigo Murders
An Alfred Hitchcock Mystery
By Dan Aulier

MURDER ON THE YELLOW BRICK ROAD

STUART M. KAMINSKY

ibooks
new york
www.ibooksinc.com

DISTRIBUTED BY SIMON & SCHUSTER, INC

An Original Publication of ibooks, inc.

Pocket Books, a division of Simon & Schuster, Inc.
1230 Avenue of the Americas, New York, NY 10020

An ibooks, inc. Book

ibooks, inc.
24 West 25th Street
New York, NY 10010

The ibooks World Wide Web Site Address is:
http://www.ibooksinc.com

ISBN 0-7434-0000-3
First Pocket Books printing May 2000
10 9 8 7 6 5 4 3 2 1
POCKET and colophon are registered trademarks of Simon & Schuster, Inc.

Cover design by Mike Rivilis
Cover photograph copyright © 2000 Richie Fahey
Interior design by Michael Mendelsohn and MM Design 2000, Inc.

Printed in the U.S.A.

To
Martin Maloney

Share your thoughts about *Murder on the Yellow Brick Road* and other ibooks titles
in the new ibooks virtual reading group at
www.ibooksinc.com

MURDER ON THE
YELLOW BRICK ROAD

It was some time before the Cowardly Lion awakened, for he had lain among the poppies a long while, breathing in their deadly fragrance; but when he did open his eyes and rolled off the truck he was very glad to find himself still alive.

—L. Frank Baum
The Wizard of Oz

1

SOMEONE HAD MURDERED a Munchkin. The little man was lying on his back in the middle of the Yellow Brick Road with his startled wide eyes looking into the overhead lights of an M.G.M. sound stage. He wore a kind of comic soldier's uniform with a yellow coat and puffy sleeves and a big fez-like blue-and-yellow hat with a feather on top. His yellow hair and beard were the phony straw color of Hollywood. He might have looked kind of cute in a Tinseltown way if it hadn't been for the knife sticking out of his chest. The knife was a brown-handled kitchen thing. Only the handle was visible.

As I stepped forward, I could see that the blood made a dark red trail down the far side of the body. The blood flowed into the cracks of the Yellow Brick Road. Up close I could see that the yellow paint was flecking off the bricks. I looked up the road. It didn't lead to Oz, but to a blank, grey wall.

Then I looked at the body and the grey wall again and wondered what I was doing here. It was Friday, November 1, 1940. It's easy to remember because the previous night just after eleven I had felt the tremor of a mild earthquake. Some Californians mark their lives by the earthquakes and tremors they experience. I just remember them and wonder how long I'll live lucky.

At the moment I didn't feel lucky. I felt stupid. An hour earlier I had been talking to someone at Warner Brothers when a call reached me. Someone said she was Judy Garland, and I should get to Metro. I got there as fast as my '34 Buick would take me, which was not very fast.

At the M.G.M. gate on Washington in Culver City I was greeted by two uniformed security men who didn't recognize me. There was no reason they should. After a few years on the Glendale police force, I had taken a security job at Warner Brothers. I'd held that for about five years and lost it when I'd broken the arm of a cowboy star. I'd propped him up a lot of times, and he let me down once too often by taking a drunken swing at me. His broken bones knocked two weeks off the shooting schedule of his latest picture and knocked me out of the studio.

Since then, I had almost made a living as a private investigator. I had met a lot of people, made almost nothing and did some freelance bodyguarding for movie people, most of whom didn't need it. I'd done some work for M.G.M. but not much and not lately.

One guy at the gate said:

"Peters?"

He was a lanky cowboy type in his fifties with grey hair and a weather-beaten face. His looks more than his ability probably carried him into his security job. I knew the route. When people did use me, it was generally for the way I looked rather than anything they knew about me.

My nose is mashed against my dark face from two punches too many. At 44 I've a few grey hairs in my short sideburns, and my smile looks like a cynical sneer even when I'm having a good time, which isn't very often. I'm reasonably tough, but there are a lot around town just as tough and just as cheap. I fit a type, and in my business I was willing to play it up rather than try to cover.

The cowboy at the gate waited for my answer. His metal name tag read "Buck McCarthy." I smiled and acknowledged my name.

"I got a call from Judy Garland," I said. "She wants to see me."

"I got the word," the cowboy said. "Slide over."

I slid over, and the cowboy got in to drive after nodding to his assistant to watch the gate. Metro was class. Two guards on a gate. I wondered if Jack Warner knew.

The cowboy switched the Buick into gear and took off slowly between the huge yellow-grey airplane hangers that served as buildings.

"You need a new heap," the cowboy said, trying to find second.

"I just had it tuned," I said. A normal man would have given up and let me drive, but he played his part to the end. No mangy Buick was going to get the better of Buck McCarthy. Buck rode my maverick past a few buildings and pulled in next to a line of low green bushes. A little man with a big hat was solemnly watering the bushes. He turned to watch as Buck stalled my car in second.

Buck glared at the little man, who was part Japanese, but the little man smiled innocently and turned back to his bushes. It was a clear day. The sun was shining and he wanted no trouble. Buck turned his glare on me. I didn't want any trouble either so I shrugged and accepted my car keys back.

Buck led the way into the cool corridors of the building, but the walk was short. We stopped at a door marked WARREN HOFF, ASSISTANT VICE PRESIDENT FOR PUBLICITY. Buck pushed the door open in front of me and a small, dark, pretty girl with glasses from the May Company basement looked up at me.

"Peters," said Buck cowboy.

The girl flicked her intercom and repeated "Peters" into it. There was the faint touch of a Mexican accent in the word. She would never get rid of that accent, but she looked determined.

"Go right in, Mr. Peters," she said. The accent was certain.

"See you, Amigo," said Buck. I waved to him as he slowly sank through the door and into the sunrise.

Hoff was advancing to meet me when I walked through his door. He was taller than I was and reasonably well built, but the build was hereditary. He didn't work at it because he didn't need his body in his work as I needed mine. He was a few years younger than I was and a dozen pounds heavier, but I could tell that I could take him. In my business, your mind works that way. It's not the most sociable way to think, but every now and then it saved a few breaks and bruises, and I can use the edge. I've had more than my share and your share of traumatized bodily functions.

Hoff shook my hand. It was firm enough and fit his

well-pressed, pin-striped suit. He didn't let go of my hand. Instead, he put his other hand on my elbow and rushed me out the door.

The girl at the desk looked up as we passed, and I sought her eyes for an explanation. Hoff wasn't even looking at me. He had the determined stare of a delivery man with a heavy bundle he wants to get rid of.

"I'm Warren Hoff," he said, turning his somewhat bland face to me with a quick smile and touching his neat brown hair to be sure it was still there.

"I'm Toby Peters," I said pulling my hand out of his grip. "And I'm not entered in this marathon."

Hoff stopped. The Japanese gardener was looking at us. He looked reasonably sane, so I gave him a nod of the head to indicate what we both thought of the insanity of a movie studio. The gardener didn't want to be my partner and turned away.

"I'm sorry," sighed Hoff, nodding apologetically, "but I think we've got to move quickly. It'll all be clear to you in a few minutes."

He didn't look like the white rabbit, and I knew too much about movie studios to think Metro was really Wonderland, but I let him lead me. I had a few dollars in the bank for a job I had just completed for Errol Flynn, but it wouldn't last long and M.G.M. was the money studio. If an assistant Vice-President was leading me and apologizing, there must be a payoff.

"Andy Markopulis told me a few things about you," Hoff said, hurrying through the lot. Within thirty yards, he was huffing and trying to catch his breath. I could tell he was not only out of shape, but a smoker. The Markopulis he mentioned was one of the M.G.M. security directors. Andy was the one who got me body jobs from time to time. Andy had been on security with me at Warners a few years back and had left for a better spot at the big studio. When I went private, he remembered me. Once in a while we had a beer, but he was a family man who lived comfortably in a house in Van Nuys.

I didn't answer Hoff. I thought he would be better off conserving his energy, but he was the nervous type who had to keep talking. He stopped hustling me across the lot long enough to take out a deck of Spuds and light one. He inhaled deeply.

That'll give you the air to go on, I thought, but said nothing. It was still a nice day. My shoes were reasonably clean, my rent was paid, and I had two boxes of cereal and plenty of coffee at home. The world was mine, and I had plenty of time.

"Come on," said Hoff, and we hurried along again. In a few minutes, after passing a bunch of brown-painted girls with bananas in their turbans, we went through the door of a big building, a sound stage. The part of the building we were in was dark, but there were enough lights to guide us past props and pieces of sawed wood. We walked around a sticky coffee spill, and Hoff took a last drag before putting out his butt. Then we plunged on into a jungle of semi-darkness.

The burst of light was sudden, like the sunrise kicking past a cloud. It came after we walked around the gigantic backdrop of what looked like a seaport. Beyond the seaport backdrop, we stepped into Munchkin City, or what remained of it; Hoff pointed at the Yellow Brick Road and the body on it. His hand urged me forward, and I moved. Only a few of the lights were on in the ceiling above us, but it was bright enough. I knew that on a set like this during the shooting of a color film, there would be enough light to make the Hollywood Bowl dazzle at one in the morning.

Hoff watched me as I stepped forward, tilted my hat back, and rubbed my chin. I didn't quite need a shave. I knelt at the body of the Munchkin and wondered what the hell I was doing here or supposed to do. I thought of informing Hoff that the little man was dead, but he seemed to know that. Other than that I had no information for him. I touched the corpse's hand; it was cold.

I looked around at the set. It was big, lots of façades of Munchkin houses and a town square with the spiral of yellow brick leading not to a backdrop of infinity but to the big, grey wall.

While I knelt near the body I said to Hoff, "I've a feeling we're not in Kansas anymore."

I couldn't tell whether the sound from Hoff was a polite laugh or the rumble of smoker's cough.

"This picture was released more than a year ago," I said, standing. "What the hell is this set still standing for? And why is this guy in costume? You making a sequel?"

"No sequel, not yet." Hoff's voice echoed through the set. He had refused to come closer than twenty-five feet from the body. "We still use some of the sets for publicity. You know, we bring visiting dignitaries and politicians here and take their picture with a Munchkin or Mickey Rooney, whichever is bigger."

This time I coughed. He must have been feeding me a standing studio joke, and I didn't want to appear out of things.

"The set will come down soon," Hoff said, "unless

we go ahead with a sequel. We'll make a decision about that soon."

Hoff included himself in the corporate "we" but I knew he wasn't high enough up to be even a small part in a decision like that.

"These sets cost a quarter of a million," he explained, "and we had to build them from the floor up. There were no standing sets we could convert. When the picture was finished, we couldn't find anything to do with them so we let most of them stand until we need the space."

That explained Hoff's control over the crumbling set, but it didn't explain anything else.

"Why is he in costume?" I said.

"I don't know," sighed Hoff nervously. "There was no publicity tour or any reason for it."

"Right," I said, but I didn't know what was right or what was going on. "Who is he, and who killed him?"

I looked at Hoff. His eyes opened a bit as his lower lip raised and his shoulders went up. It was an enormous response of non-information. He didn't know either answer.

"O.K.," I said giving the body a last look and being careful not to touch anything. "Now, what the hell is going on here?"

Hoff gave an enormous sigh and collapsed into a chair from which he could see the entire lighted set. There was a chair next to him. I sat in it, and for a minute or two we looked at the remains of Munchkin City and the remains of a single military Munchkin. We were just like two old friends enjoying the sunset. All we needed was a couple of beers and the football scores.

"Miss Garland reacted in panic," Hoff said, finally

fishing out another Spud and taking a long time to light it. He didn't want to make any mistakes in what he said. He was acting as if his career were on the line, and maybe it was. "She discovered the body and called you."

"Why me?" I asked.

"She remembered your name from yesterday," said Hoff, his eyes fixed on the Munchkin to be sure he didn't suddenly rise and walk off. "It had been mentioned at a party. It seems you were spoken highly of by someone at Warner Brothers. We didn't find out she had called you until just after she hung up."

"Why didn't she call the cops?" I asked, also watching the dead Munchkin.

"She has been working very hard since *Oz*," Hoff explained very carefully and slowly as if he were practicing a press release. "I—we—think it has gotten to her, that she needs some rest. She just wasn't thinking too clearly."

I have learned that it's sometimes a good idea to wait out a client or a suspect until he talks himself out, into a corner or into a frenzy. The corporate Hoff, however, was abusing the privilege of either client or suspect.

"Mr. Hoff . . ." I began.

"Call me Warren," he smiled, fishing out another Spud.

"Warren, if you want me to just turn around and leave," I said, "I'll be happy to do so, and I'll forget I ever saw our little friend over there." Warren Hoff winced at the words, but I went on. "When I'm gone, you can shovel the body under the road, cart it off somewhere, or call the cops. All you'll have to do is pay me $25, my expenses for a day, and say good-bye after

I confirm all this with Miss Garland. She called me and I'd like to see her before I leave. Now I don't have many principles, but..."

"We know a few things about you," Hoff interrupted, pulling out a small, blue notebook from his matching blue jacket. He glanced at the book and spoke.

"You have a reputation for discretion, Mr. Peters..."

"Call me Toby," I said.

"You know something about M.G.M. and have done some work for us," he went on. So far it was all true, but he hadn't come to the punch line. Then he did: "And you have a brother, a Lieutenant Philip Pevsner, who is a Los Angeles Homicide detective."

I shook my head and smiled. He noticed.

"Is that information wrong?"

"No, it's right," I said, "but where you're heading is wrong. You want me to talk to my brother about keeping this quiet, conducting a nice, silent, publicity-free investigation."

"Well," he began, "we..."

"Who is this 'we,' Warren?" He winced again, probably not too happy that I'd taken up his offer to call him Warren or question his corporate identity. It equalized us too much. The studio was his, but I knew more about death than he did. "I have no influence with my brother; less than none. You see this nose? He's broken it twice when I've gotten in his way. You'd have a hell of a lot more influence with my brother than I would."

I started to get up. "I'd like to collect some Metro money," I said, "but I don't see how. No offense, but it's a little late to guard that body, and a lot too late for me to ask a favor of my brother."

Hoff looked confused. The word must have been that I could be bought cheap and easy. Normally, the word was good, but this was out of my league. I'd just spend a quiet afternoon at the Y, and then listen to Al Pearce and the Loyola-San Jose State game on KFWB. I'd snuggle up with a bowl of shredded wheat and a Rainer Beer and think about my next weekend date with Carmen, the plump, widowed waitress at Levy's. The plan seemed great to me, and I turned my back on the dead Munchkin.

"Wait," said Hoff touching my arm. "You want to see Judy? I'll take you to her."

I nodded. Things were going badly for Warren Hoff, and I felt sorry for him, but not too sorry.

"Warren, if you want my advice, call the cops and say you just found the body."

There was a plea on his face, but the look on mine cooled it. He shrugged enormously again and led the way out past the coffee spill, away from the seaport and back into the light. He didn't say anything, didn't even pause to light a Spud. The temperature was about 70, but sweat stains were showing under the armpits of his jacket. I wondered if he was high enough in the company to have a couple of extra suits in his office.

I couldn't figure out if Hoff was so confused that he was lost, or if he knew a super shortcut to wherever we were going. We dodged a truckload of balsa lamp posts, stepped through a small town street which I recognized as Andy Hardy's Carvel, and backed up as an assorted group of convicts and Apache Indians hurried past.

We finally stopped at a row of doors leading into a squat, wooden building.

"Judy starts working in *Ziegfield Girl* tomorrow,"

Hoff explained, his hand hovering over the door handle. "She's got a tough schedule, and we don't want her bothered too much about this."

"I'll just kiss her hand, get her autograph on my back, and leave," I assured him.

"You know what I mean," he said.

"I know what you mean," I answered. I wanted to put my hand on his shoulder and tell him to take it easy. There were plenty of jobs at Columbia and 20th Century for a good M.G.M. reject.

"And I used to play football," he said softly.

"That a fact?" I said, not knowing what to say. The statement didn't seem to make sense, but I had the odd feeling that I understood why he was saying it. I didn't exactly like him, but I was closer to understanding him. He knocked at the wooden door and a feminine voice said, "Who is it?"

It wasn't Judy Garland's voice.

"Warren," said Warren Hoff. His voice had dropped two octaves to confident baritone. The woman told us to come in, and Warren underwent a transformation as he pushed the door open. He became a different man, taller, smiling, and full of quiet confidence.

When we entered the room, I found out what the transformation was all about. Before us, in the dressing room, stood a dark, beautiful woman. She was wearing a black sweater, a knit skirt, and a slight smile behind the most perfect soft mouth that I had ever seen. Her eyes were narrow, almost Oriental. For some reason there was a tape measure around her neck. I found out the reason when Warren Hoff introduced us.

"Cassie James, this is Toby Peters, the man Miss Garland called," he said. I noticed that Judy had become

Miss Garland. "Cassie is a costume designer and a friend of Miss Garland's."

Cassie James extended her right hand, and I took it. It was firm, warm and tender. Up close she was a few years older than she had looked from the doorway. I guessed her to be about 35, a perfect 35. I released her hand before she could see the excitement building in me. The same hormonal response was bursting out through Warren Hoff's pores.

"Is Miss Garland here, Cassie?" Hoff said showing a beautiful double row of near-white teeth. He was clearly a Kolynos toothpaste man. What was their ad? "Now you can make your teeth look their romantic best."

I never knew what I was brushing my teeth with. I used samples the drug company salesmen gave to Sheldon Minck, the dentist I shared my office with.

"Judy took a ... something to calm her nerves," Cassie James explained softly. "I think she's sleeping."

"No, I'm not."

The voice came from the other side of a high-backed, flower-decorated sofa in the corner. Judy Garland sat up and looked sleepily at the three of us.

Cassie James stepped over to her and took her hand.

"This is Mr. Peters, Judy," she explained. "The man you called."

The name rang a bell, and she brushed some of the sleep from her eyes. She stood up and tried a weak smile, but I could see that something had gotten to her, probably the dead Munchkin. She was several things I didn't expect. I had seen the little girl in *The Wizard of Oz*. It was the same person, but she was not a little girl. She was also shorter than I expected, no more than 5'2", and her clothes were definitely not little girl's clothes.

She wore a white fluffy dress with a big patent leather belt, and her hair was built up on her head to make her look taller or older or both.

"Mr. Peters," she said taking my hands. The voice belonged to a more familiar Dorothy of Kansas, but it was filled with sadness and pleading. I wanted to hold her and tell her everything was going to be all right. If she cried, and she looked as if she might, I probably would have turned into a fool running around looking for a handkerchief.

From the corner of my eye I could see Hoff sliding his way to Cassie James's side. He was looking at Judy Garland, but the body warmth was going to Cassie James. I didn't feel sorry for my pal Warren anymore.

"I'm sorry if I've caused you any trouble, Mr. Peters," Judy Garland continued, that near sob in her voice, "but I panicked. You know how that can happen? I . . . Cassie and I saw him lying there, and I just turned and ran to the nearest phone and called information. They gave me your office, and a Dr. Minck told me you were at Warner Brothers and I just . . ." She shrugged, gulping in air, and led me to the sofa. We sat while she held both of my hands tightly and looked into my eyes. My God, there was a tear forming in one eye. In another second, I'd be lost.

"You knew the dead man?" I asked.

She shook her head in a decided, sad no.

"To tell the truth, Mr. Peters," she said softly, "I . . . I didn't even like most of the little people who worked on the film. They like to be called little people, you know, not midgets or dwarfs."

"I didn't know that," I said, noticing that Cassie James was listening to our conversation with concern, and that Hoff was so close to her I couldn't tell if they were touching. "Why didn't you like them?"

"Oh," she said, "I didn't dislike all of them, just some of them. One especially who kept touching me and asking for dates and saying things. I . . ."

"O.K., O.K." I said. "You saw the dead Munchkin, and you felt glad and guilty. I've seen a few dead ones, and my first reaction was always, I'm glad it's not me. The second reaction is to feel queasy in the stomach. Cops, hospital people, and some soldiers get used to it, but the rest of us feel lucky, sick, and guilty."

"I guess it was something like that," she said taking a deep breath. "Mr. Peters," she began, and then turned her head toward Cassie James. "Cassie, could I please talk to Mr. Peters alone for a minute?"

Cassie James showed a slight smile of perfect teeth and an understanding turn of her head as she led a pleased and confident looking Hoff outside and closed the door behind her. Hoff was one hell of an actor for a PR man—inside, he was filled with fear for his six-figure job, but to look at him now you'd think he was William Powell.

My attention turned back to Judy Garland, who was watching my face.

"She's beautiful, isn't she?" the girl-woman said.

I thought about lying, pretending I didn't know what she was talking about, but I also felt that I didn't have to.

"She is," I said.

"I wish I could be beautiful like that," she sighed.

"You are beautiful, and you'll get better," I said.

"Mr. Peters, I am not a fool." Her voice was stronger now, waking up. "I'm a plain 18-year-old girl who can sing. As my mother says, I've got the talent, but not the looks. I'm playing a woman for the first time in *Ziegfield Girls*, and we start shooting tomorrow. You know who I'll be with in that picture? Lana Turner and Hedy Lamarr. Any beauty *I've* got has to be put there by make-up, lights and experts."

"You're underrating yourself," I said, uncomfortable with the role of confidant to a teenager. Besides, who was I to give advice on beauty? On a good day, I could pass for the steady loser in tank town five-rounders.

She looked at me steadily, and almost whispered, "I got a call to go to that set. Someone called this room and told me Mr. Mayer wanted me to get over there fast for some publicity shots with Wendel Willkie."

"Wendel Willkie?" I said. "He's in . . ."

"Camden, New Jersey," she finished. "I know that now, but I didn't until I just saw the newspaper. Cassie checked. No one from Mr. Mayer's office told me to go to that stage. No one from publicity called me to go to that stage. Mr. Peters, someone just wanted me to be the one who found that body. Why would they do that?"

Her big brown eyes were examining my face for an answer. I didn't have answers, only questions.

"Was the voice male or female?"

"Male, but a little high I think. I didn't pay too much attention at the time."

"O.K.," I said. "Did you recognize it—the voice?"

"I don't think so."

"He called you here?" She said yes.

In a few minutes, I discovered that Cassie James had been in the dressing room with her when the call came, that Cassie had not talked to the caller, that she had accompanied Judy to the Munchkin set, and they both had discovered the body. According to Judy, Cassie James was a good friend and a kind of mother figure for her, though Cassie James didn't look motherly to me. Judy's own mother, I picked up from a few remarks, was not the girl's favorite person. It seemed reasonable, or so I told myself and Judy Garland, that I should talk to Cassie James before I decided what to do. In the course of the few minutes we talked, whatever she had taken wore off. She stood up and moved to the door, telling me that she felt well enough to go back to a *Ziegfield* set where they were rehearsing around her.

She opened the door and looked back at me.

"I'm all right now, Mr. Peters, but I am scared and I'd like your help."

She left before I could tell her that I had no help to give. I could hear the two women exchanging words outside the door, and Cassie James came back in without Warren Hoff.

"Warren's gone out to get help, someone to make you come to your senses and take this job," she explained with a smile that kept me from standing. "Would you like something to drink?"

It was about ten in the morning, and I didn't drink anyway except for an occasional beer. I said no, but accepted when she offered coffee.

The coffee was already made and warm in the corner. She poured us both cups and sat next to me.

I shook my head.

"You don't remind me of anyone," I said, "I was trying to think of something smart to say to get you laughing."

"I don't laugh easily," she said, gliding over the compliment. She obviously had a lot of experience bypassing double-meaning compliments. I dropped it and turned to business.

In about five minutes, Cassie James confirmed what Judy Garland had said, and added that she had been friendly with the actress for about a year or two.

"I did a little acting," she said, getting up for more coffee. I watched her. "But, after a few years, I could see I wasn't going to make it. I have some ability—" she shrugged "—but I couldn't take it. When you're an actor, you're yourself and someone else at the same time. People criticize the face you were born with, dissect your emotions, complain about your posture, praise the moments you like least, ignore the instant you feel perfect pain."

"You're quite a person," I said.

"Thank you," she laughed, and then the laugh died.

"I had a younger sister who could have made it through," she said with a slight pout, "but she died. Maybe that's why I'm feeling rather motherly about Judy. She reminds me of my sister."

I was stumbling around in my head for something to say to make the next move with her, but nothing came. She had, as the toughs in Warner films said, "class," and I couldn't quite bring myself to invite her to my place for cereal and a night of radio listening. My place was a single room and a bath in a neighborhood where you don't bring people like Cassie James. I decided to try anyway, but Hoff came into the room without knocking.

He looked at Cassie and me to be sure there was nothing going on. He wasn't quite satisfied, but he held his confident look.

"Mr. Mayer would like to see you, Peters."

I looked at Cassie, who raised her eyebrows in mock respect. I gave a knowing shrug as I rose to follow Hoff.

"Be seeing you," I said.

"I hope so," she beamed, and I hoped she wasn't just being polite.

Hoff sulked ahead of me, his confidence drooping as soon as the door closed. I tried to adjust to the prospect of seeing the boss, the final "M" in M.G.M., the most important person in the movie world. Hoff didn't give me the chance to adjust.

"What were you two talking about, Peters?"

"I'm Toby, remember, and you're Warren." I hurried along at his side. He had changed into another suit, but if he kept drooping and hurrying and smoking, he'd go through a whole wardrobe before lunch.

"What were you talking about?" he demanded.

"Shove it up your ass, Warren," I said. It may have blown my $25 in expenses, but a man has some pride and I was still remembering the scent of Cassie James.

Hoff turned in mid stride and faced me, probably remembering his football days when he had run over linemen or tackled cheerleaders or whatever the hell he did. We stood glaring at each other for a few minutes like two twelve-year-olds in the schoolyard who won't back down.

"Warren, either take a swing at me or lead the way to Mayer's office. I have other ways of getting exercise."

A fat man in a cowboy suit passed us slowly, stalling a bit to see if we would start slugging. Hoff turned suddenly at the sound of Mayer's name and hurried on.

Entering Mayer's office proved to be something like going to see the Wizard in his chamber. Hoff stopped at a door and announced me to a beautiful blonde in a pink dress. If she had a desk, I couldn't see it. The blonde escorted me through a door and turned me over to a deskless redhead who finally took me to another beautiful blonde who had the distinction of having a desk. Blonde Number Two led me down a carpeted corridor, and just as I had resigned myself to endless wandering around the building led by beautiful women, we stopped at a door and she knocked.

From somewhere in the distance a voice answered, "Come in."

The blonde opened the door and backed away. I stepped into an enormous room. The walls were white with a few pictures. The distant desk was white. The chairs and sofa were white. It looked like a plush padded cell. On the far end of the big room, behind the desk, stood a short, spectacled man with a prominent hooked nose, who appeared to have no neck. He wore a grey suit and a serious look. As I came closer, I could see that his hair was a well-trimmed grey, and he seemed to be somewhere in his mid-50's.

I had to lean across the desk to shake his hand. He took my right hand in both of his and held it tightly.

"I'm Louis Mayer," he said, "and you are Toby Peters."

I knew that already, but if the man with the highest salary in the world wanted to remind me, I was happy to listen.

2

I LOVE THIS country," said Louis B. Mayer, waiting for an argument. His voice was faintly New York, and he seemed sincere enough. "What do you think of this country, Mr. Peters?"

"I love it," I said.

He kept looking at me with suspicion. I adjusted my blue tie.

"Herbert Hoover says we're far more likely to be drawn into the European War under Roosevelt than Willkie, and Willkie says the United States is sick of the type of government that treats our Constitution like a scrap of paper," Mayer said, lifting a crisp copy of the *L.A. Times* from his desk in evidence. "I think Mr. Hoover is right. What do you think, Mr. Peters?"

"I think this has nothing to do with a dead Munchkin," I said, smiling.

"You get smart with me and I'll throw you out!" shouted Mayer, dropping his newspaper on the floor.

"You'll need a lot of help," I said, relaxing or pretending to. The white chair I was in was covered with fur, and damned comfortable.

"I can get help," said Mayer.

"I'm sure you can."

We stared at each other for a few more years, and Mayer decided on a new strategy: the story of his life.

"I came to this country from Russia with my family when I was four years old. My father was a junk man, and we moved around America from New York to Canada and back again. My father, who was nothing but a laborer in Russia, became a successful ship salvager in the United States. When I was fourteen, I became his partner. Do you know what day I was born on?"

I admitted that I didn't.

"I don't know either," he said, putting both hands on his desk. "So I picked my own birthday: the Fourth of July. That's how I feel about this country. When I was a kid, I bought a little movie theater in Haverhill, near Boston, for about $1,000. That was in 1907. Eight years later, I owned a bunch of theaters and was making my own movies for them. I've got a motto, Mr. Peters. I've always had this motto. Do you know what it is?"

I was getting tired of not being able to answer questions M.G.M. people put to me, so I tried, " 'Always be prepared'?"

"No, Mr. Peters," he said solemnly. " 'I will make only pictures that I won't be ashamed to have my children see.' Do you see where we are going?"

It was gradually getting through to me, but he went on.

"*The Wizard of Oz* is a clean picture. Judy Garland is a wonderful girl, like my own child . . . like Mickey Rooney is almost a son to me."

Like they make you millions of dollars, I thought,

but even as I thought it I could see that Mayer was, in an odd way, sincere.

"A scandal connected with the studio, with that movie, with Judy would be bad for the country, Mr. Peters. People believe in that picture, believe in us. If I thought it would help, I'd get down on my knees to you." He clasped his hands in prayer and his eyes searched my face. His eyes glazed over moistly.

"The truth is, Mr. Mayer," I said getting up, "I've got nothing you want to buy."

"Not true, Mr. Peters." His right hand came out and pointed to me. A smile was back on his face. "You have some influence with the police. You have a reputation for discretion."

Everyone at M.G.M. was reading the same script on me, and it was still wrong.

"My brother won't listen to me," I explained.

"A brother is a brother, Mr. Peters."

I couldn't argue with that.

"And besides," Mayer continued picking the *Times* up off the floor and laying it neatly on his desk, "you want to help Judy. She's a sweet girl. I'd do anything for her. You know about the Artie Shaw problem?"

I said I didn't know about the Artie Shaw problem. Since I didn't, he had no intention of telling me.

"What is your fee, Mr. Peters?"

"$35 a day and expenses," I said.

Mayer smiled. His head shook.

"Your fee is $25 a day without expenses," he chuckled. "We'll give you $50 and expenses."

"To do what?"

He held up his fingers as he ticked off my duties.

"Try to persuade your brother to keep the investigation quiet. If any M.G.M. personnel are involved, do your best to keep that quiet, too. You're a bodyguard, right? You also act as Judy Garland's bodyguard until this is taken care of."

"And if I don't keep the investigation out of the papers?"

Mayer shrugged. "You're fired."

It seemed fair enough, so I took the job. Mayer and I didn't shake hands. He turned his head back to some papers on his desk.

"I think I've already said more than I have to say," he said.

Taking that for dismissal, I plodded my way out of the white, fur-padded auditorium he used for an office, made my way down the corridor of smiling beauties, and found Warren Hoff waiting for me with a pile of ashes in a tray next to where he sat. He got up quickly. His hair was not neatly in place.

"God says I get $50 a day, expenses, and a lot of cooperation."

"You'll get it," said Hoff.

We walked back to Hoff's office. On the way, we passed Walter Pidgeon talking to a short, chunky woman in big glasses. Pidgeon was laughing heartily and saying, "That's priceless."

"Mr. Mayer is very persuasive," said Hoff without any sarcasm.

"He convinced me it was my patriotic duty to help M.G.M.. If I don't work for M.G.M., we'll be at war with Germany within a year."

I wasn't sure what had convinced me to take the job. The money was good. I did want to provide some fatherly protection for Judy Garland, and by taking the job I stood a good chance of seeing Cassie James again. The only problem was that I didn't think I could come near to doing what I was to be paid for. I pointed out to Hoff that I had one day's pay coming already. He paid me out of his wallet as we walked.

The small, dark girl with the Mexican accent and May Company glasses looked up as Hoff and I entered his office. Hoff looked terrible. He had sweated through another suit and run out of Spuds. The girl looked concerned, but we swept past her and into Hoff's office.

While I phoned the L.A. police, Hoff poured himself a small drink of something from a bar hidden in a cabinet. He didn't offer me anything.

I got past the switchboard operator and made my way to an Officer Derry. He wondered why I wanted to talk to Lieutenant Pevsner. No one who knew Phil Pevsner could understand why anyone would willingly seek his company. I used my full real name, Tobias Leo Pevsner, to cut through the blue tape and indicate I was the man's brother. It got me to Sergeant Seidman, my brother's partner.

"Toby," said Seidman coming on the phone, "he doesn't want to talk to you, and if you're smart, you won't want to talk to him. We've had a tough week."

"Sergeant, I'm reporting a murder. Someone's murdered a Munchkin at M.G.M."

There was silence at the other end, except for the background sounds of typewriters and cops talking.

"You want me to tell your brother that?" he said calmly.

"It's true. Why don't the two of you come . . ."

There was a crackling sound at the other end and

the clunk of the phone, then my brother's rumbling voice:

"Toby, you fuck-up. If this is one of your stupid jokes, you'll do hospital time."

He meant it and I knew it, but I couldn't resist. Maybe it was a death wish or something.

"How are Ruth and the kids?" I asked. For some reason, maybe the fact that I never visited him and his family, this always drove Phil up the wall, and the walls of the L.A. police department are no fun running up. Besides, with the gut he was developing, a run up the wall was out of the question. He hung up.

"Will he come?" Hoff asked finishing his drink.

"He'll come," I said, leaning back and putting my feet up on the desk. I picked up his newspaper and began to read, trying to look as confident as I was not.

It took fifteen minutes for Phil and Seidman to get to M.G.M. In that time I discovered through my reading that the Greeks had hurled back an Italian invasion, that the Japanese were charging that Americans were assembling arms at Manila, that the A&P was celebrating its 81st anniversary, that I could get a suit from Brooks on South Broadway for $25 and take three payments, and that a bottle of FF California port could be had for 37 cents.

The call came to Hoff's office from cowboy Buck McCarthy at the gate. Hoff told Buck to take the police to the Munchkin City set, and then he hurried to the door. I slowed him down and told him it would be a good idea to let the police get to the scene first. I folded the newspaper neatly, placed it on Hoff's desk and got up. I was in no hurry to see Phil Pevsner. The only one who had ever successfully stood between us in battle was my dad, a Glendale grocer, who had died a long time ago. There were a couple of times even when he was alive that Phil almost lost control and went for me right over our father. Dad would have been flattened like a beer can in the Rose Bowl parade if Phil hadn't gotten himself under control. It had been something I had said, but I couldn't remember what it was.

When Hoff and I got to the *Oz* set, we walked in slowly, like a camera dollying in to the center of a Busby Berkeley musical number. Three people stood looking down at the dead Munchkin, who had not moved nor been moved. Two of them, Seidman and my brother, wore badly rumpled suits. The third guy was a big, bald, uniformed cop I recognized as Rashkow. Rashkow was only in his twenties, but heredity and my brother had robbed him of most of his hair. Seidman turned to me and Hoff with a sour look I recognized. Seidman was thin and white-faced. He hated the sunlight. Phil just looked at the corpse with anger, as if the little man had purposely conspired to ruin his day. For Phil, Los Angeles was strewn with corposes whose sole job was to complicate his life and make it miserable. He hated corpses. He'd even kicked one in anger once, according to Seidman. He hated murderers even more. The only thing he hated more than corpses and murderers was me.

Phil was a little taller than me, broader, older with close-cut steely hair and a hard cop's gut. His tie always dangled loosely around his neck, and his face frequently turned red with contained rage, especially when I was present. M.G.M. had certainly picked the right guy to calm him down. By the time Hoff and I were within five feet, Phil's lower lip was out, and his head was gently shaking up and down like a bull building up for a charge.

STUART M. KAMINSKY

Seidman pulled out a notebook. I nodded to him and to Rashkow, who was afraid to smile.

"Toby," Phil began plunging his hands into his pants pockets to keep them calm," "I'm going to ask you questions, and you are going to answer without jokes. Then you are going to get your ass out of here. You understand?"

I understood and said so. I was determined to keep from irritating him.

"Who found the body?"

"I did," I said. Hoff twitched next to me.

"Who's he?" Phil asked, nodding at Hoff, "and what's up his ass?"

"His name is Hoff," I said. "He's an assistant vice president for publicity. I was supposed to meet him here about working as a bodyguard for a premiere when I stumbled on the body."

"I see," said Phil, starting to walk in a small circle on the yellow brick road. "You were meeting on this set instead of in his office because it's more comfortable and convenient here."

"He wanted to keep our meeting secret," I said slowly, "because the star I was assigned to doesn't like protection."

"That right, Hoff?" Phil said, moving no more than two inches from Hoff. Sweat popped out of Hoff's pores.

"That's right," Hoff said softly.

"It's bullshit!" Phil shouted in Hoff's face. The shout had enough impact to send Hoff staggering back a few feet with numbed ear drums. "What's going on here? Who killed the little turd?"

"Phil, we don't know," I said with my hands coming open and palms up. "I just stumbled on the body."

"Who is he, the dead midget?"

"They like to be called 'little people,' " I corrected.

"He doesn't give a shit what we call him!" Phil shouted. "Who is he?"

Everyone looked at Hoff.

"I don't know," he said. "There were a few hundred little people on the picture. He might not even be one of them."

"Well," sighed Phil, putting his hand on Hoff's shoulder, "do you think you could get someone in here to identify him? And then can you round up anyone who has been in this building in the last twenty-four hours and will admit it?"

Hoff said he could, and Phil told Rashkow to call for someone from the Coroner's office. I thought of the Coroner from Munchkin City who had certified the death of the first Wicked Witch. He had stood right about where Phil was standing.

"What was the dead midget doing in here?" Phil asked Hoff. "And why is he wearing that costume?"

"We don't know what he was doing in here and why he was wearing his costume," answered Hoff. Phil looked at Hoff as if he were useless, and Hoff reached for a Spud. Seidman got Hoff's office number and sent him on his way to get possible witnesses. Seidman and Rashkow began to look around the set, and Phil turned his back on me and walked over to the waterless Munchkin City fountain where he sat looking dyspeptically at the corpse and the set. He took a white tablet out of his pocket and popped it into his mouth. He chewed it furiously. Little pieces of it spat out when I approached him and sat down.

"You're a goddamn liar," he said, chewing away.

I shrugged.

"Phil, can you think about keeping this quiet for a while?"

He stopped chewing and looked at me blankly. I waited for the blank look to turn to rage and expected his thick hand to catch me before I could move away, but the look turned to a smile, and then a laugh. Both Seidman and Rashkow stopped to see what had happened. Phil almost choked with maniacal laughter. In the midst of his laughter, he grabbed my collar and stood up. Our noses were almost touching when he spoke.

"Toby, I've messed you before and I'll do it again. You're covering and you're trying to use me. You didn't have to call me for this. Don't use me, brother. I don't like it, and don't play me for a fool. Don't mistake a bad temper for stupidity. You've done that a few times in the past and what did it get you?"

"This nose," I said. He liked the answer and let me go.

"You covering for somebody?" he said, sitting again.

"No," I said, trying to unwrinkle my shirt. "But bad publicity on this thing could ruin the image of the picture, cause the studio trouble. No one's asking you not to investigate, not to do everything. But you let this out and the newspapers will be driving you crazy, too. They'll be on your back. You want that?"

"You're concerned about me," he said. "I'm touched."

I hadn't expected my argument to do any good. My next move was going to be to suggest he talk to Mayer. Maybe Mayer's double-talk, power, and sincerity would get to Phil, though I doubted it.

"I'll think about it," he said.

I almost fell in the dry fountain in surprise. He looked away from me.

"You know you've got two nephews, Toby," he whispered angrily, "and one of them, Davey, the older boy . . ."

"I know Davey's your older boy," I said. He gave me a look of contempt, and I suddenly had the image of Davey and Nate, his kids, pounding on each other the way Phil and I had.

"Davey just got out of the hospital," Phil went on. "It was close."

I knew that, too, and he knew I knew, but I kept my mouth shut. Phil's wife, Ruth, had told me once that Phil was a good father. I wasn't sure what that meant. He certainly wasn't like *my* father.

"In their room," said Phil, "the kids have a poster from the movie. They saw it five times. I don't want to be the one who tears down that poster."

"Thanks Phil. I . . ."

He turned, boiling slowly.

"I didn't say I wouldn't do it," he explained. "I said I don't want to, and you have nothing to thank me for. I never wanted your thanks or asked for it."

That was true. I shut up. It surprised me how closely Phil's and Mayer's philosophy were to each other. Phil said I could go after I gave a statement to Seidman, which I did. Seidman also gave me a statement. Phil owed a lot of money to the hospital. Ruth was blaming him for not being around enough. It was what cop's wives did. It was their duty to complain. Eventually, it was their duty to stop complaining or walk out. My wife walked out. I didn't think Ruth would, but you never know.

Hoff wasn't in his office when I got there, but I left a message with his secretary that it looked as if I could keep the lid on for a few days. I gave her my office number and listened to her worry about Hoff for a few minutes before I escaped.

I eased my Buick into gear, coaxing the pistons with sweet thoughts, and made my way past the Japanese gardener and around an elephant being led by a girl with very little on besides a few spangles. At the gate I waved good-bye to Buck McCarthy, who had his thumbs in his pockets, cowboy style. It was my turn to drive off into the sunset, but it was only a little after noon.

I stopped at a Mexican place for three tacos and a Pepsi and headed back to my office.

3

WITHIN TWO HOURS I had met a dead Munchkin, consoled Judy Garland, argued with Louis B. Mayer, and got a job with M.G.M. It was the kind of news you ran home with to your wife, your mother and father, or your dog. I didn't have any of them, but I did have Shelly Minck.

Shelly and I shared space in the Farraday Building on Hoover near Ninth. The Farraday had the eternal smell of Lysol to cover up the essence of derelict in the cracked tile hall. Sometimes the neighborhood bums slept it off under the stairs until the landlord, a gentle gorilla of a man named Jeremy Butler, plucked them up and deposited them in back of the building. Butler had been a professional wrestler. Since he retired after investing in real estate, he had devoted himself to plucking bums from his lobbies and writing poetry. Some of Butler's poems had actually been published in little magazines with names like *Illiad Now* and *Big Bay Review*.

Butler was in the lobby plucking a bum when I arrived. He nodded to me and headed to the rear of the building. His footsteps echoed away, and I felt at home as I went up the stairs. There was an elevator, but a crippled spinster on relief could beat it to the fourth floor without even trying.

I hiked up the stairway past three floors of offices belonging to disbarred lawyers, bookies, second-rate doctors, pornographic book publishers, and baby photographers. Far behind, I could hear Gorilla Butler dumping the bum and closing the fire door.

Chipped letters on the pebbled glass door to my office read:

SHELDON MINCK, D.D.S., S.D.
DENTIST
TOBY PETERS
PRIVATE INVESTIGATOR

I opened the door and carefully avoided the pile of outdated magazines on the table in the alcove we called a waiting room. The waiting room had two chairs that had come with the place before Shelly moved in. One of the chairs had once been covered with leather. Someone had knocked over the room's lone ash tray. The alcove wall was decorated with an ancient drawing from a dental supply company showing what various gum diseases look like.

I pushed open the inner door and entered the office of Dr. Minck. Clients for me had to pass through his office where he was often working on a neighborhood bum or a raggedy kid. I had rented the office space from Shelly after I did a small job for him. We got along, and he let me pay what I could afford, almost nothing.

Shelly had a stubbly-faced bum in the chair. The

bum looked like a startled old bird. No, he looked like Walter Brennan imitating a startled bird.

Shelly—short, fat, in his fifties, and desperately myopic—was humming and puffing on his ever present cigar while he tried to read the label of a small bottle over the rim of his thick glasses. When he heard me, Shelly turned and nodded a greeting with his cigar. He was, as always, wearing a once white smock which had stains of both blood and jelly on it. Shelly didn't introduce me to his patient. Walter Brennan just popped his eyes open and darted them between me and his dentist. I couldn't see a tooth in the guy's head.

"Any calls?" I said.

"No calls, some mail," replied Shelly, satisfied with the label on the bottle. He turned to his patient and patted his head reassuringly with the same hand in which he held his cigar.

"Mr. Strange here and I are engaged in a mission of mercy," Shelly said, plunging a hypodermic into the bottle in his hand. Reddish liquid burbled into the syringe. Shelly pointed to the old man's mouth with the needle. "Mr. Strange has a toothache. We know exactly which tooth it is because Mr. Strange has only one tooth. That right, Mr. Strange?"

Mr. Strange gave a birdlike nod of agreement. He was petrified with fear, but Shelly didn't seem to notice.

"We are going to save that tooth, aren't we, Mr. Strange? We are going to perform something called a root canal. We are going to do it because one tooth is better than no teeth, and because I have not performed a root canal in some time, and I need the practice. Now open up, Mr. Strange."

Shelly shifted the cigar in his mouth and forced the

old man's mouth open with his strong, sweaty fingers. The hypo plunged in and the old man gurgled.

"That'll kill the pain," whispered Shelly. "Now we'll just let that go to work for a little while."

While we were waiting for the shot to work on Walter Brennan, I told Shelly about my morning at Metro. He listened while he groped around for an instrument he wanted. He found it underneath some coffee cups in a corner. Then he went to work on the old man. Above the sound of the drill he said, "I worked on a midget once. Little tiny teeth, but the *roots* on 'em. That little cocker had roots like steel. Two extractions on that midget were harder than a mouthful of root canals. Try to hold still, Mr. Strange. This will only take twenty or thirty minutes."

Having failed to impress what passed for my only friend, I went into my office. I'd save the story of encounters with the great and near great for my date next week with Carmen.

My office had once been a dental room. It was just big enough for my battered desk and a couple of chairs. The walls were bare, except for a framed copy of my private investigator's certificate, and a photograph of my father, my brother Phil, and our beagle dog Kaiser Wilhelm. The ten-year-old kid in the picture didn't look like me. His nose was straight. He was smiling and holding onto the dog's collar. The fourteen-year-old looked like Phil, with the dark scowl, the tension. The tall, heavy man in the picture had one hand on each kid's shoulder.

There wasn't much mail on the desk. Someone in Leavenworth, Kansas wanted to send me a catalogue of tricks and novelties for a dollar. A client named Merle

Levine who had lost her cat wanted me to return the ten dollar advance she had given me. The case was two years old. I hadn't found the cat. I hadn't really looked. Two brothers named Santini on Sepulveda wanted to paint my home or office for a ridiculously low price.

I wrote a note to Mrs. Levine and put three bucks in it, telling her that it was an out-of-court settlement. Then I leaned back to listen to Shelly's drill as he hummed "Ramona." Through the window I could see Los Angeles—white, flat, and spread out. The skyline from my window wasn't much. Since 1906, a municipal ordinance had limited buildings to 13 stories. Someone at City Hall hadn't heard about the law and the City Hall Building was 32 stories high, but most of the buildings in the city were low. The skyline was a series of long, low lines like other American cities threatened by earthquakes and a lack of solid rock under them.

The phone rang. It was almost two o'clock. Shelly answered it and said it was for me. I picked it up, while I fished through my drawers for a stamp to mail the letter to Mrs. Levine. The caller was Warren Hoff. He had news.

The police had a suspect, a midget who had been in *The Wizard of Oz*. The midget's name was Gunther Wherthman. He had been known to fight with the dead Munchkin, who was now identified as James Cash. In fact, the two little men had been arrested during the shooting of *Oz* in 1939 when they had a knife fight in their hotel. Wherthman had been cut by Cash, and the police had records showing that Wherthman had threatened to kill Cash. The police had also found three witnesses who had seen two midgets arguing violently before the murder outside the stage where Cash's body was found. The witnesses all described one of the midgets as wearing a Munchkin soldier's uniform. The other midget was described as wearing a Munchkin lollipop kid costume. Wherthman had, according to Hoff, played one of the lollipop kids in the movie. Hoff's report was good.

"I used to be a reporter before I got into this," he explained.

"Maybe you'll go back to it," I said.

"It's too late," he said. "Once you commit yourself to a bigger income and lifestyle you're hooked."

It wasn't a problem I'd ever had to deal with.

"Then that's it," I sighed, thinking about the easy fifty in my pocket and slightly regretting the other fifties I might have had.

"Not quite," said Hoff. "We want you to talk to Wherthman, find out if he's guilty, keep trying to hold back on the publicity. If Wherthman did kill Cash on the lot and both of them were in costume, we'll look terrible."

"Is this your idea?" I asked.

"Hell, no," gasped Hoff. "I think we should just drop the goddamn thing and let it ride out. M.G.M. isn't going to fold over this. *Oz* has already had its run. It's not even playing anywhere now, and I doubt if there ever will be a sequel. But Mr. Mayer says there are millions to be made from the picture, re-release and . . ."

"And what?"

"Television," Hoff said sounding embarrassed. "He thinks we'll be able to sell it to television someday."

Not knowing what television was, I didn't say anything, but I grunted in sympathy for Hoff. I agreed with him. I had nothing against putting in another few days' work for the money, even if I didn't expect anything to come of it.

"O.K. Warren," I said, pulling out an unsharpened pencil. I bit wood away to get to the lead. "I'll put some more time into it. I'll try to get to Wherthman. Who are the witnesses, the ones who saw the two midgets fighting this morning?"

"One is Barney Grundly, a studio photographer," said Hoff. He gave me Grundy's office address on Melrose. "The other two are Victor Fleming and Clark Gable. They were coming from breakfast together. If you want to talk to Fleming, I'll find out where he is. Your brother already talked to him and Gable. Gable's going out of town for the weekend, but I'm sure we can track him down if you want him."

I said thanks and told him he had done a good job, which he had. My praise didn't mean much to him. We hung up.

I didn't know where to look for the midget suspect Wherthman, so I called Steve Seidman at police headquarters. He told me Wherthman had been brought in for questioning, but it was a pretty sure bet they were going to hold him for the murder. As far as the L.A. police were concerned, the case was just about wrapped up and they could turn their attention back to a pair of ax murders in Griffith Park.

Shelly was still working on Walter Brennan when I put on my hat and stepped through my office door.

"I think we've saved it," Shelly beamed, sweat dripping from his hair. The old man in the dental chair was having trouble focusing his eyes.

"Great," I said. "You're a saint."

On the way down to try to get a word with Wherthman, I realized that Mayer had a few reasons to worry about publicity. The primary witnesses for the case against Wherthman seemed to be the studio's top star and top director. Coming off of *The Wizard of Oz* and *Gone With The Wind*, Fleming was almost as great publicity material as Gable. A trial would be front page news for weeks. As far as M.G.M. was concerned, it would probably be better if Wherthman would just confess and plead guilty. Wherthman, however, might not care much about Metro's publicity problems.

Wherthman hadn't been charged or booked when I got to the station. Phil wasn't there, which was fine with me; Seidman was, and he told me that the little suspect was just about wrapped up and ready to be put away.

"A couple of people saw Wherthman arguing with Cash, the dead midget, early this morning," Seidman explained. "One of the witnesses got close enough to hear them talking. He heard a German accent. Wherthman's got a German accent. The dead guy called the other guy 'Gunther.' We found blood on a suit in his apartment. We're checking it now to see if it matches the dead guy."

"He sounds all wrapped up," I said. "Can I talk to him?"

"Why?" Seidman asked reasonably.

"I've been hired by his lawyer."

"He hasn't called a lawyer. Who's his lawyer?"

"I'm not at liberty to say," I said seriously.

Seidman smiled and shook his head.

"Phil would have your head in a Christmas stocking if you fed him that crap."

We looked at each other for a few minutes. Behind us, cops were scurrying around the big, dirty, wooden room, which was about twenty degrees warmer than the outside. Two were drinking coffee and had their heads close to a thin black kid. The cops' faces were gentle and they were whispering, but whatever the hell they were whispering was scaring the hell out of the thin kid. A couple of detectives were on phones, and two guys were handcuffed together and sitting on a bench waiting. One of the guys had no shirt on, but he was wearing a tie. He looked content if not happy. The other guy slouched and tried to act as if he had nothing to do with the shirtless smiler. The sloucher had a massive bruise over his right eye.

"You can see him," Seidman finally said. He was feeling generous. He had helped crack a murder in less than three hours. It would look good on everyone's record, including my brother's. Seidman's face oozed confidence.

He led me to my brother's office, and I walked in. The office was a small cubicle in one corner of the big squad room. The noise from the cops and robbers was barely muffled by the thin wooden walls. There was enough room inside for the battered desk, a steel file cabinet, and two chairs. On one of the chairs sat a little man whose feet didn't touch the floor.

Wherthman wore a light grey suit and dark tie. His hair was dark and slightly mussed. He had a little black mustache and a fresh red bruise on his right cheek. I could guess who put it there. His face didn't look young, but it was hard to tell. I guessed he was about my age.

"Mr. Wherthman, I'm Toby Peters."

I put out my hand. He didn't move his, and I put mine down.

"I told the other policeman that I had nothing to do

with this murder," Wherthman said. His voice was high and his accent was clear and Germanic. Not only did the cops have an assful of evidence against him, he looked like and sounded like a miniature Hitler. With war fever running high and Roosevelt running on a fear campaign to keep us out of Europe, Wherthman would be about as popular in Los Angeles as another earthquake.

"I'm not a policeman," I said, sitting next to him so that the difference between us wouldn't be quite so ridiculous. "I'm working for your lawyer to help you."

He looked puzzled.

"I have no lawyer."

"You will as soon as I call a friend at M.G.M.," I said softly. The room wasn't bugged, but Seidman was probably standing outside the door to find out what the hell I was doing.

"Why should anyone at M.G.M. want to help me?" Wherthman said evenly. It was a damn good question.

"They don't like the publicity," I explained, and before he could question it I went on. "And besides, can you afford a lawyer and do you know one?"

He said he didn't know a lawyer and had little money. The pay for *Oz* was long gone and he had been getting along by doing translations from German for a project at The University of Southern California. He added that he wasn't German, but Swiss. I didn't think most Americans would recognize the difference.

"Why did you kill Cash?" I asked.

"I did not kill him," Wherthman said, looking up at me. "That is what I told the policeman, the fat..." he groped for a word to describe Phil, but his English failed him.

"Pig?" I tried. Wherthman liked it.

"Yes, pig. He threatened to step on me. He hit me. Can the police do that? Can they hit someone in this country?"

"They may not, but they can and do," I explained.

Wherthman thought it over for a few seconds and indicated with a shake of his head that he understood the distinction. I was beginning to like him.

"The evidence is pretty strong," I said. "You were seen talking to Cash this morning. You've fought with him in the past. You've threatened him. The police found blood, probably his, in your apartment."

"I have no apartment," he corrected. "I have a single room in a boarding house. I did not go to the studio this morning. I took a walk early as I always do. Perhaps witnesses could be found who saw me. Several people no doubt did."

"Do you know any of their names?" I asked. "Anyone you see regularly?"

He didn't know any names and couldn't think of anyone he saw regularly. He couldn't explain how a witness had heard Cash use his name. He couldn't explain why someone would be using the costume he wore in the movie. He couldn't explain how blood got on some of his clothes in his room.

"So you think you've been framed?" I concluded.

He looked puzzled.

"You think someone is trying to make it look as if you committed this murder," I explained.

"Yes, of course," he said. We sat for a few seconds listening to a deep voice outside the office thundering over the general noise. The voice told someone to sit still or lose an arm.

"Why would anyone want to do that, Mr. Wherth-man?" I asked.

"I do not know," he said, "but it is being done."

"How well did you know Cash?" I tried.

Wherthman shifted slightly and slid forward so his toes would touch the floor. His shoes were worn but nicely polished.

"I knew him better than I would have wanted," he said. "We were forced to live in proximity when the movie was being made. We were placed in adjacent rooms in the same hotel. He was ill-mannered and vulgar. He provoked me because I had an accent, was educated and taller than he. Even with my accent, my English was more precise than his. Precise is the proper word, is it not?"

"It is the proper word," I said.

"Did he fight with any other little person?"

"I see," said Wherthman, "Yes. Perhaps someone of my size is attempting to blame me."

"I don't know how many little people there are around Los Angeles," I said, "but there can't be a whole hell of a lot, and the list of those who knew Cash and the studio well enough to get a costume this morning must be even smaller. Finding a patsy would be a good idea."

"Patsy," he mulled. "I thought this was a female name?"

"It is, but it's also a kind of slang for someone to take the blame for something you did."

Wherthman took all this seriously. I could see him storing it for future use.

"That would be the Canadian," said Wherthman. "The one with the nasty temper. He also did not like me

44

and was a confidant of the one called Cash. I think 'confidant' is the right word for they were not friends, but they were much together, sometimes arguing, sometimes fighting. They spoke of going into some business together when the movie was finished."

"What was the Canadian's name?" I asked.

Wherthman couldn't remember. He gave me a vague description, but I needed more. It wasn't a great lead, but it was something. I asked him to try to remember the name, and he said he would.

"Don't tell the police anything more," I said, reaching out my hand. He took it this time. His hand was small but not soft, and his grip was firm even though his fingers barely reached past my palm.

"I will not," he said, standing.

"They're going to charge you with murder and book you. Tell them your lawyer will be in touch with them. And I have another bit of advice. Shave that mustache. It makes you look a little like Hitler."

His finger went up to his face.

"I did not think of that," he said. "I have no wish to look like Hitler. I will do as you suggest. Mr. Peters?"

He had only heard my name once and in a tough situation, but it had stuck.

"Mr. Peters? Do you believe I did not do this murder?"

"I believe it," I said, "but I've been wrong before. I'll be in touch."

There was more confidence in my farewell than I felt. Not only had I been wrong before, I've been wrong most of the time about my life and other people. The only people who felt any confidence in me were a myopic, sloppy dentist and a Swiss midget.

Seidman was pretending to read a report on a clip-board right outside Phil's door.

"He says he didn't do it," I told him as I walked through the squadroom. The handcuffed couple was still there, and the shirtless guy adjusted his tie as we passed.

"He sticks to that and we'll wind up with a trial," shrugged Seidman. "You know who some of our wit-nesses are?"

I told him I knew.

"Now that'll really be publicity," he said. "Might be a good idea if his lawyer or someone..."

"Like me?" I said.

"Someone," continued Seidman, "suggested that he plead guilty. We have other things to work on, and this can be handled quietly."

"It's a thought," I said. "Thanks for letting me talk to him, and give my best to Phil."

"I'll tell him you were sorry you missed him," Seid-man said, getting in the last crack. His white face looked pleased, and I had nothing more to say. As I walked out, the thin black guy between the two cops drinking coffee put his head in his hands and leaned forward. It looked like he was going to throw up.

I stopped at a Pig 'n Whistle on the corner and had a burger and Pepsi. I liked the "Pepsi and Pete" ads the company put out with the two comic cops. When Coke came up with something better, they'd regain my gour-met trade. While I waited for my sandwich, I called Warren Hoff and told him what had happened. He said he'd get a lawyer for Wherthman. I didn't ask him what the lawyer would tell the little man, but I doubted if they could get the little guy to confess to the murder.

The next step was to talk to the witnesses and try

to get a lead on the Canadian midget with the bad temper, so I asked Hoff where I could reach Fleming and Gable. I already knew Grundy's address. Hoff had the information in front of him.

"Victor will be having dinner at the Brown Derby tonight. He'll get there around six, and he's been told that you might drop by to ask him a few questions. Clark is spending the weekend at Mr. Hearst's ranch in San Simeon. If you want to talk to him by phone, he should be arriving there soon. He drove up."

I noticed that Fleming and Gable were Victor and Clark but Hearst was Mr. Hearst. Even Hoff realized how silly it would have sounded for him to say that Gable was at William Randolph's or Willie's or Bill's.

"Thanks," I said. "I'll be in touch."

He gave me his home phone number in case I wanted to reach him later in the evening, and I let him hang up first.

I spent another nickel and called M.G.M. again. This time I asked for Judy Garland and gave my name. I got her on the line in about thirty seconds. She said she was finished for the day.

"The person who called you this morning and told you to go to the *Oz* set. You said it was a man with a high voice."

"That's right," she said.

"Could it have been a midget?"

She said it could and I asked the important question.

"Did he have an accent? You know, Spanish, French, German?"

"No, no accent."

"Thanks," I said. "I'll get back to you. Tell Cassie I said hello."

"I'll tell her, she's right here." She laughed and hung up. She had a hell of a nice laugh. Either Wherthman had a helper, or someone unconnected with the murder called Judy Garland, or Wherthman was right, and he was being framed. It wasn't evidence to go to the cops with, but it gave me a little confidence in what I was doing.

I ate my burger and headed home.

Home until a month earlier had been a walkup near downtown and my office and a long trot to the Y on Hope Street. But my former landlady had taken exception to a difficult night in which the apartment was shot up and a guy who was trying to kill me went through the window. I couldn't blame her too much, and it wasn't hard to move. My clothes, food, and books fit nicely into two cardboard suitcases I got for almost nothing in a pawnshop on Vermont. The pawnbroker, a guy named Hill, owed me a favor for catching a thief who was robbing him blind during the day. Cameras, radios, binoculars, watches had been missing every day at closing time. I staked myself out under a counter with a couple of sandwiches and watched the store between two boxes. The thief turned out to be the seventy-one-year-old lady who brought Hill his lunch from the deli across the street. Hill always ate standing in the store so he wouldn't lose business. She did all her grabbing on the way out, dropping things into the shopping bag she used to deliver Hill's food. She hadn't resold or used any of the stuff. She had just stolen it for the excitement. It was piled up in her room down the street. Hill had paid me, but four hours under that counter with my bad back had me laid up in bed for a week. He felt guilty, and I used that guilt to get things from him, like the suitcases and the .38 automatic owned and never used. It was the second .38 I got from Hill. The first one had been taken by the cops after a guy took it from me and killed a couple of people with it.

That was old business. New business was the place I was living in on Long Beach Boulevard near Slauson. It was small and cheap, partly because the place had the smell of fast decline. It was one of a series of two-room, one story wooden structures L.A. management people called bungalows. To people passing by, the place looked like a motor court that had lost its license and sign. Paint was peeling from all the houses in the court like the skin from a sunburned, aging actress. Like the actress, the bungalows were functional, but not particularly appealing. When it rained, the ground in front of my place became a swamp. The furnished furnishings were faded and the shower didn't work, but it had a great advantage: It was cheap. Jeremy Butler, the poetic wrestler who owned my office building, also owned this place and suggested that I move in and keep an eye on the property for him. In return, I paid practically nothing in rent. A few days earlier I had paid with a sore stomach when I caught a kid trying to break into one of the bungalows at night. The kid had butted me with his head and taken off. His head had hit the point where I had recently taken a bullet, and the wound had just barely scarred when the kid hit it.

When I pulled the Buick in front of my place, it was about four in the afternoon. The Sante Fe moaned, rattling the walls, and I went inside, kicking off my shoes at the door. Through the thin walls I could hear a couple with hillbilly accents arguing, but I couldn't make out the words.

I ran the water in the bath full blast. Full blast meant it would be about three-quarters full in half an hour. The half hour was spent getting coffee and pouring myself a big bowl of Quaker Puffed Wheat with a lot of sugar. I finished the Puffed Wheat while I took a bath and read the comics. It was the day before Sadie Hawkin's Day, but I was sure Li'l Abner would be all right. I ran through Mary Worth's Family and Tarzan, and got happy for Dick Tracy. He said he was going on vacation.

I put on a pair of shorts, plopped on my bed, and listened to the radio for about an hour with my eyes closed. By a few minutes after six, I was dressed in my second suit and ready to go. Such was the domestic life of Toby Peters, which suited me just fine most of the time.

The hillbilly couple were still arguing when I left, but they weren't breaking anything so I ignored them and got into my Buick. When I was a kid, my father and brother and I always named our cars. Since my dad's car was always a heap, we needed a new one every year or so. I remember one was called Valentino, a Model A Ford. I'd thought about naming the Buick, but nothing seemed right for it. I decided to ask Butler. As a poet, he might have some ideas. I took Long Beach to Washington and went up Normandie heading for Wilshire.

It was on a stretch of Normandie near some factories that the bullet missed my head. The street was pretty well deserted, but a car pulled up behind me and gave me the horn to get out of the way. I didn't even look in the rear view mirror. As the car passed, my neck began to itch, and I started to turn. The bullet went through the driver's side window near my nose and right out the opposite window. I hit the brakes, held the wheel and ducked down below the door. My tires hit something and the Buick spun around and stopped. I didn't have my .38 with me. I crouched over, listened for a few seconds to be sure the other car had gone. When I sat up, the street was clear and the sun was still shining. The holes in both windows were small, but they sent out rays like the sun in a kid's drawing. I rolled the windows open so no one would ask about the holes.

Then, I headed back to my place and got my .38. It was getting late for my meeting with Victor Fleming, but I needed some solid reassurance. It could simply have been a nut. There are plenty of nuts in Los Angeles, especially kids who are looking for dangerous thrills. There is something about the monotony of L.A. that sometimes drives people mad. Maybe it's coming to the ocean and finding there is no place further to take your life. It was also possible that an enemy had been laying for me. I had a few old enemies and some recent ones. It was also possible that it had something to do with the dead Munchkin. That seemed just as wild, since I didn't know anything the cops didn't know. Or did I? I went over everything in my head as I drove, keeping my eyes open for another attack. I came up with one idea. Late or not, I had to check it out. I stopped at a gas station and called my office while a guy with a Brooklyn Dodgers cap and an old, grey sweater gave me half a buck's worth.

Shelly was still in the office. He wanted to talk about his root canal, but I didn't have the time and he sounded a little hurt.

"You had a call, Toby," he said, accepting temporary

defeat. "A guy with a high voice. Said he wanted to hire you and had to get to you fast. So I gave him your address. Did he find you?"

"He found me, Shelly, thanks." I found out the caller had no accent and told Shelly I'd see him when I could.

It didn't make sense, at least not to me. I dropped it, after deciding to bill the cost of new car windows to M.G.M., and headed for the Brown Derby. It was almost seven when I got there. I found a space a few blocks away and jogged. The Derby was a greyish dome with a canopy in front and a single line of rectangular windows running around it. Perched on top of the dome and held up by a tangle of steel bars was the replica of a brown derby. The place looked something like an erupted boil wearing a little hat.

I told the waiter that Fleming was expecting me and was led to a table in a corner. The room was jammed but the noise level was low.

Fleming got up and shook hands when I introduced myself. He was a tall guy, about sixty, with well-groomed grey hair. His nose looked as if it had taken one in the past. He was wearing a tweed suit, a checkered tie and a brown sweater. He looked very English, but his voice was American.

"Have a seat, Peters," he said. There was another guy at the table and Fleming introduced him as Dr. Roloff, a psychiatrist.

Roloff was equally tweedy and even more grey than Fleming, though about ten years younger.

"Dr. Roloff has been kind enough to give me some ideas for my next picture," Fleming explained. "A version of *Dr. Jekyll and Mr. Hyde*."

I must have looked surprised because Fleming

added, "I know it's been done with Freddie March. A good film, but I have some ideas and Spencer Tracy is interested. But that's another game. What can I do for you, Peters? Can we get you something to eat?"

"Nothing to eat, just some information and I'll get out of your conference. The police talked to you today about an argument you saw between two people dressed in Munchkin suits."

Fleming nodded and I went on.

"What exactly did you see and hear?"

"Very little," said Fleming, taking a belt of coffee. "I was coming back from breakfast with Clark Gable, and we saw the two little people arguing. Clark looked. I wanted nothing to do with it. I had a year of working with them. Most of them were fine, but a lot of them were a pain in the ass. They argued, disappeared, showed up late. Once they screwed up a take on purpose by singing 'Ding Dong the Bitch is Dead.' I didn't notice it. The sound man didn't notice it. We had to reshoot it."

"It's not surprising," Roloff put in. "Short people, midgets especially, are sometimes inclined to be highly aggressive toward normal size people. They're also inclined to use obscenity more than the average to assert their adultness, to overcompensate. I had one midget as a patient who knew he was overcompensating with big cigars and sexual overtures to full-sized women. He knew he looked ridiculous and obscene to others, but he couldn't stop. It was a kind of self hate, a punishment for himself. It's hard to live your life knowing that whenever you go out on the street people will stare at you. Exhibitionism may result, or the person may become a shy and bitter recluse."

"Just like movie stars," I added.

"Sure," said Roloff.

"Sorry I can't help you, Peters," Fleming joined in. "I can give you a lot of stories about Munchkins, but I don't think it will help. It just supports what Dr. Roloff has been saying. I'll give you an example. One of them got drunk one day and almost drowned in a toilet. Another time one of them pulled down his drawers in a crowd scene. We didn't even notice that the first time through the rushes. As for the fight this morning, when I saw it was two little people in Munchkin suits, I paid no attention. I stepped in between them a few times when we were shooting the picture, and I had no desire to take the abuse again. When I saw those two this morning, I didn't know why they were wearing costumes from the movie and I didn't give a Hungarian crap."

He paused to look around the room and regain his composure. The thought of the Munchkins had sent his temper flying.

"I like what we did on that picture," he continued, patting down his hair. "I came in on it late after a couple of other directors, and I was pulled off it early to take over *Gone With The Wind*. Still, I spent more than a year on *Oz* and it was the toughest damn thing I've ever done. Those two pictures have been damn good for me, but I wouldn't want to make either one of them again. Even if no one remembers *Oz*, I will, and with mixed memories."

"I like it," I said.

"It's a strange movie," said Roloff, pushing his cup away and fiddling with his pipe. "Depending on who views it and what's going on in his or her life, it can be a lot of things."

"Like what?" I asked.

"It's a child's dream of accepting the adult world. A girl at puberty dreams of seeking the aid of a magical wizard, aided by three male figures, each not quite a man. Her jealous rival is an old witch who wants the slippers the girl wears. The ruby red slippers can be seen as a menstrual sign. In the book they were silver. The girl in the movie learns to accept power of the ruby slippers—her womanhood—with the help of three flawed male admirers and a mysterious, frightening father figure. The slippers are given to her by a mother figure, a beautiful witch. Did you ever think of having her wake up and find she's had her first period, Victor?"

Fleming laughed.

"I had no such interpretation in mind when I made the movie, and neither did anyone else who worked on it," Fleming said.

Roloff lit his pipe and puffed a few times. Then he raised his hand.

"That's just the point I was making about the Jekyll film," he said. "It doesn't matter if it is consciously in your mind. A dream doesn't necessarily have a conscious meaning. You simply tell the story because you find it interesting and others do, too. My job is to find out why you find it interesting and what it means."

"You said there were other interpretations," I said.

"Well," Roloff said, "how about this one? A lot of people may be reacting to the film as a kind of parallel to the current world situation. If we see the Munchkins as the Europeans—foreign, different, in need of help—and the witch as Hitler, we have a situation in which an All-American girl is forced to take up arms against evil, to help the innocent foreigners, to destroy the well guarded militant Hitler-Witch and to be rewarded in her effort by the human-father-God, the Wizard of Oz."

"But it turns out to be only a dream," Fleming said shaking his head and motioning to the waiter for more coffee. This time I took some.

"Right," said Roloff. "It's just a dream, to a great extent a nightmare with a happy ending. The film says if we have to enter the war, we will, and we will triumph to return from it as if from a dream. Perhaps we will have to face the fear of death in a colorful and far off place before we can return to the dull security of Kansas. In any case, the message might simply be, if we have to handle it, we can. Would you like another possible meaning?"

I smiled and said two were quite enough, and Fleming said if we weren't careful, colleges would start teaching courses about the "meaning" of movies. What Roloff said was interesting, but I didn't see any way I could use it. I was wrong, but I wouldn't find out till it, was almost too late. As far as I was concerned, the meeting with Fleming provided nothing.

"Sorry again I couldn't be of more help, Peters," Fleming said. "Clark paid some attention to the incident, and he has a hell of a memory. He might be able to give you more."

I said good-bye to Roloff and Fleming and left the Derby. It was after nine. I stopped at a stand for two tacos and a chocolate shake.

A year, several thousand memories, and a dozen broken bones ago I had seen *The Wizard of Oz*. It had been on one of those nights when I was feeling sorry for myself. There had been nothing on the radio and nothing to read. I decided to see the movie again. I wanted to try to pick out Cash and Grundy, wanted to look at Judy Garland and see if she had changed as much as I thought.

I stopped at a newsstand and got a *Times*. The picture wasn't playing anywhere. I was going to give up, and head home, but I didn't want to think about what or who might be looking for me at home. I had to see *The Wizard of Oz*.

I called Warren Hoff at home. He answered and told me I didn't need to see the picture. I suggested that he handle the publicity business and I'd handle the detective business, and both of us would probably meet at the funny farm. He said he'd set up a screening in the morning. I pushed, for the moon was high, my blood was up, and I had no lead to follow.

"Wait," said Hoff. "I've got an idea." He put the phone down, and I looked out of the booth at a thin blonde woman in a grey suit. She caught me looking and stared me down. I pretended to start talking even before Hoff came back.

"Right," I said.

"What's right?" said Hoff.

"I don't know," I said. "What did you find?"

"There's a charity screening of the picture tonight." I could hear him crunching through some papers. "I've got a list of extra screenings on . . . here it is. Holy Name Church of God's Friends in Van Nuys, on Van Nuys just South of Victory."

"I know the place," I said. "What time?"

"Nine-thirty. Enjoy yourself." He hung up.

I drove in the dark, listening to the end of the San

Jose-Loyola game. San Jose won 27 to 12, and a back named Gene Grady ran ninety-seven yards for a touchdown.

The church was where I remembered it. A few years before, I had waited for a bus outside of that church for an hour, listening to a skinny woman with a red wig tell me her life story. It was a hell of a sad life. I remember her face when the rain came down in the middle of her tale about a draining liver.

"See?" she had said, shaking her head knowingly. The rain had been another proof of the hell of her life. She didn't seem to notice that the rain was falling on me, too.

The Holy Name Church of God's Friends was a four-story red brick building with a big sign. When I stepped through the thick wooden doors I could tell what kind of church it was. The ceiling went up about ten feet and I didn't see any second floor. The front of the church was a façade, a store front, a prop to make it look as if the church went up four stories, three closer to God than the truth. I wondered who the people of the church were trying to fool, God or the street trade. I didn't much care.

A guy with a thick, white, turned-around collar greeted me at the door. He had red cheeks and messy white hair. He looked like a priest.

"You're a little late," he whispered. "The short is already on."

I gave him a nod and headed for the door in front of me and behind him. He touched my hand gently.

"We would appreciate a donation to the church," he said humbly.

"And if I don't want to give a donation?"

"Well," he whispered, "I'll just call a few people and throw your ass out of here." The benevolent look never left his face.

I smiled and coughed up a buck. He took it and stuffed it in his pocket.

"Enjoy the movie, son," he said.

"Thank you, Father," I said.

"No," he corrected. "In this church I am called Friend. Friend Yoder."

I left him standing in the hall and stepped into the dark room. I couldn't see much except the beam of light from the projector and restless shadows. The projector grinded, feet shuffled, old women coughed, and a baby revved up for a hell of a cry.

The short was an English thing about a train carrying mail to Scotland. I watched for a minute or two while my eyes got used to the dark. An English narrator was reading a poem about postal orders. It sounded kind of sing-songy. It had something to do with carrying mail and how great it was. I found a wooden seat next to a woman holding a kid who couldn't have been more than three. The kid decided to look at me instead of the picture. I couldn't tell if the kid was a boy or a girl, but I could tell that someone should have wiped his nose when he was two.

I played goo with the kid till the picture ended. The lights went on and I could see the place was crowded, mostly with old people and a couple of women with kids falling asleep or trying to get away from the arms that held them. I moved to another seat near the front and the kid at my side whined. The old man next to me smiled. I smiled back, and the picture started.

The old man chuckled when the Bert Lahr character

Zeke told a pig to get in the pen before he made a dime bank out of him. No one else chuckled. Things picked up when Dorothy got to Munchkinland. I recognized the set and the soldier costume on a bunch of midgets marching. They all looked the same to me.

When the Wicked Witch said, "Just try to stay out of my way," the blond kid with the nose let out a scream of terror. His mother told him to shut up.

In a few minutes, Dorothy observed that, "People come and go so quickly here." It was the problem I was facing.

The blond kid got uncomfortable again when the trees talked, and I got uncomfortable when the Scarecrow observed that, "Some people without brains do an awful lot of talking."

I got sleepy when the group hit the poppy field and felt like going home when the movie ended with Dorothy saying, "There's no place like home." Then the lights went on and I remembered where I lived.

I dodged past old people and women with kids and nodded to Reverend Yoder as I pushed open the front door and went out onto Van Nuys.

When I reached home thirty minutes later, I locked my door, pulled down the shades, propped a chair under the doorknob, and put my .38 under the pillow. It wasn't likely that a reasonable killer would break in here and take a few shots at me, but it was possible that a murderous midget who knew my address might just be wild enough to try it. For some reason, the prospect of being shot by a midget scared me more than the idea of the same thing being done by a normal-size man. What if the little killer crept in through a crack under the door and plunked a knife into my chest? I could see the dead soldier Munchkin and me lying side by side on the yellow brick road.

I had a hard time getting to sleep, so I left the light on in the bathroom. It had worked when I was a kid, and it helped now. No one would ever know. The radio was glowing next to me and singing softly. My hand felt the comforting steel of the .38 under my pillow, and I fell asleep expecting nightmares.

There were no nightmares. I dreamed I was sleeping peacefully in a field of poppies, and snow was falling coldly and gently on my face.

4

THE RADIO WAS purring music softly in my ear, and a band of light was dancing across my face from a slit in the shade of the single window in my living room/bedroom. I felt like turning over for a few more hours, but I had a busy day planned and fifty bucks to earn, probably the hard way.

I turned off the radio and padded my way to the bathroom carrying my .38. I kept the gun on the toilet seat while I brushed my teeth and shaved with a Gilette Blue Blade, the sharpest edge ever honed. I cut myself twice. After coffee and a mixed bowl of puffed rice and shredded wheat, I looked up an address in the phone book, got dressed, plunked my .38 in the holster inside my jacket, pushed my hat back at what I considered a rakish angle, and went out into the sun.

My hillbilly neighbors had stopped feuding, and the day was clear. There wasn't enough time to get my windows fixed, so I left them rolled down and headed for the office of Barney Grundy, the photographer who had witnessed the fight between the two midgets at Metro the morning before. I got to the corner of Melrose and

Highland without anyone trying to kill me and found a parking spot a block from where I was going.

Grundy's address was on a doorway between an auto parts store and a travel bureau. His place was up the stairs behind a door marked B. NIMBLE GRUNDY, PICTURES STILL AND MOVING. The lettering was in pink against a yellow square. I knocked, prepared for almost anything, but I wasn't prepared for what opened the door. He was about six-foot-three, with bleached, yellow hair that would have been called white on an older man. He wore a blue tee shirt and black slacks, and was drying his hands with a small towel. He was deeply tanned and remarkable. He looked like a caricature of Tarzan. His muscles were enormous and bulging with veins. His tee shirt could hardly contain him, which was probably why he wore it. I thought of asking if there was a man inside the mannikin before me, but I wasn't sure if he would take it as a joke, and I didn't want to get started on the wrong foot.

"Barney Grundy?" I asked.

He put out his hand and grinned. It was an infectious boyish grin, and his grasp was firm but not bone-breaking. I had a feeling that he was holding back out of politeness. A second look told me he wasn't as young as he first appeared. I would have taken him for mid-twenties with a first look. I added ten years to the estimate on second look.

"You must be Peters," he said, standing back to let me in. "Mr. Hoff told me you might want to talk. Come on in."

I came on in. There were photographs on the wall in the wide room. The wall was filled with them. Most of them were women, big prints, framed and mounted.

I recognized a few of the women as movie stars and almost stars. There was no carpet on the finely polished wooden floor, and the furniture was minimal. The room was clean and bright. Three stairs led up to another level that looked like a combination living room/bedroom, and kitchen. There were a couple of doors beyond it where I guessed he did his work.

"Hey, listen," Grundy said in a soft tenor. "I was on the way out to get some breakfast. You want to come with me?"

I said yes, and he put his towel carefully over a chair and led the way out.

"You're in good shape," I said as we went down the stairs.

"I work out every day for an hour or two with weights in a place down in Santa Monica," he explained, leading the way out. "There are about a dozen of us. It's a kind of competition to see who can develop the best muscle tone."

We walked down Melrose to LaBrea and I asked, "Don't you get musclebound?"

"No," he grinned. "That's something made up by people who don't know what they're talking about. I can run a six minute mile, touch my nose with my big toe, and please ladies. You look like you're in fair shape yourself."

"Y.M.C.A.," I said. "I run a little and play handball."

I didn't add that my total miles per week had dropped to five and my handball partner was a sixty-year-old doctor who was well ahead of me in games, but a damn good player.

Grundy led me into a coffee shop on La Brea, and we sat in a booth. The waitress recognized him, and he flashed her a smile. She was an overworked, washed-out creature with frizzy hair. The smile from Grundy made her day.

We ordered, and I asked, "Why do you do it?"

"Body build?" he said, "Compensation in a way, Mr. Peters. It started when I realized that I wasn't going to make it as a camera operator or cinematographer with a studio. That was what I wanted. I was born a few miles from here. I've passed those studios all my life. I wanted to be behind a camera, even prepared by becoming a still photographer, taking movie courses. But it never happened. I never got the break. I guess I started the weights when I knew it wasn't going to happen. No one has said I'm not good enough. Maybe I'm just the right guy in the wrong place."

"So," I continued, "you make up for it by doing stills for studios when you can get the work and building your body."

"That's about it," he agreed, welcoming his plate of four fried eggs and half pound of bacon from the waitress who smiled at him while she served. She had forgotten my coffee, but went back for it quickly.

"Most of my work is baby pictures and some industrial stuff," he explained between bites. "Once in a while I get to do spillover work for a studio or a small industrial movie, nothing much; but I live cheap and do all right."

He was telling me more about himself than I needed to know, but I've run into a lot of people like that. They'll give you their life stories and a cup of Hill's Brothers if you'll just sit and listen. I'm a good listener. It may be the thing I'm best at.

"About yesterday, the morning?" I asked.

"Right," he said, finishing a glass of milk in a long gulp. "I was in the studio to deliver some pictures I'd taken and walked past these two midgets arguing."

"How close were you?" I asked. The coffee was bitter, but I kept drinking.

"About ten feet," he said. "Walked right past them. I told the cops. I heard them arguing, and one of them had an accent, a German accent. The other one, the one in the soldier suit, called him 'Gunther.' That's all I heard."

"Could you identify either of the midgets again?" I tried.

"No," he said, finishing his toast and looking around for something else to eat. I thought he'd give the plate a try, but instead he motioned to the waitress who knew what he wanted and brought more milk, toast and jam. "Both the little guys were wearing makeup and costumes, and I didn't really look at them. I was tempted to break them up, but they weren't actually fighting and it was none of my business."

"Weren't you surprised to see them in *Oz* costumes?"

"No," he said with a shake of his head. "I know they still do occasional publicity shots with the midgets. I've even taken a few myself for Mr. Hoff. The midgets get a day's fee for posing and so do I for a few quick prints."

"Did you see anyone else when you passed the arguing midgets?" I'd finished my coffee and had a refill before I could stop the waitress, who was happy for any excuse to come back to our booth and gawk at Grundy.

"No, no one else was in sight," he said. His fresh order of toast was gone and he wiped his mouth with a napkin.

"Last question," I said reaching in my pocket for money. "What time did this happen?"

"A little after eight, maybe a quarter after at the latest. Hey, I'll take the check."

He reached for the check but I pulled it out of his reach. He had reached fast. He may have had muscles like blocks of wood, but they didn't slow him down.

'I'm on an expense account," I explained. "Breakfast is on Louis B. Mayer."

He knew how to accept a free breakfast graciously. I paid the moonstruck waitress and walked back down Melrose with Grundy.

"My car's down here," I said. We shook hands. "If there's anything else I can do, let me know," he said. "And if you ever need any photo work in your business, here's my card. I'll work cheap."

The card read exactly like his door: B. NIMBLE GRUNDY, PICTURES STILL AND MOVING. It also had his address. I thanked him and watched him jog toward his office-home.

It was Saturday and Grundy looked like a man who owned Saturdays. The day wasn't quite mine, though. Either Grundy was lying, which wasn't likely, or the midget who killed Cash had faked a German accent. In which case, why had Cash called him "Gunter"? The other possibility was that Gunther was guilty. Or maybe Gunther had fought with Cash but not killed him. In which case he had simply lied to me, for which I couldn't much blame him.

My leads had almost run out. All I had left was Gable and the hope that Wherthman would remember the name of the other midget who had worked and fought with Cash. Both were slim. Something had to make sense, and I was heading in the right direction or there wouldn't be two bullet holes in my Buick.

Judy Garland had told me production was starting on *Ziegfield Girl* today so I headed for the studio. It wasn't far from Grundy's place. I took another look at his card and put it away, reminding myself to ask if Nimble was his real middle name if I should ever see him again.

It was a little after ten when I arrived at the studio. Buck McCarthy was on the gate and he sauntered over to me, chewing a wad of gum and pretending it was a plug. He leaned into the window.

"Miss Garland said to hurry you in if you showed up," he said. "You know the way?"

"Yep, you want to drive?"

He declined this time, and I drove slowly to her dressing room. I didn't see any stars, but a group of carpenters working on the fake front of what looked like the Taj Mahal. The fake front was leaning against a real building.

Judy Garland wasn't in her dressing room, but Cassie James was, which suited me fine. Today she was dressed entirely in pink with a red patent leather belt. She smelled like July in the mountains. When I knocked and came in she was pouring herself a cup of coffee from the pot brewing in the corner.

She gave me a small smile and handed me the cup. Something was wrong. She sat in a straightbacked chair and crossed her legs.

"Someone tried to kill Judy," she said.

For a second or two I didn't absorb the words. Maybe I even thought I imagined them, but I hadn't.

"Tried to poison her," Cassie continued.

"How? When?" I sat with my coffee on a chair a few feet from Cassie.

"When we came in the morning, there was a pitcher of ice water on the table. Judy was a little nervous about starting the picture today and her throat was dry. I poured her a drink and started to hand it to her, but it looked a little discolored. I smelled it, and it smelled strange. So she didn't drink it."

"Then how do you know it was poisoned?" I asked.

"We called the doctor. There's one on hand when-ever shooting is going on. He said it was filled with arsenic. A mouthful would very likely have killed Judy."

Cassie was certainly nervous, but not in panic.

"It's lucky you noticed," I said reassuringly. "Where's Judy now?"

"She's shooting. I told her to take the day off and wait till we talked to you, but she wouldn't do it. She got sick once during the shooting of *Oz* and held up shooting for a while. She doesn't want to do it again."

Cassie gave me more information. The dressing room door hadn't been locked so anyone on the lot could have come in with the water. The poison water had been dumped out after the doctor confirmed the presence of poison. It wasn't clear whose idea the dump-ing was, but no one had questioned it. The pitcher was glass, but with everyone handling it there probably wouldn't have been worthwhile prints anyway.

"O.K.," I said, standing up and putting down the cup. "I think we should call the police. Someone tried to kill me yesterday, too."

She got up suddenly and looked shocked. I was touched.

"What happened?" she asked, stepping toward me.

"Someone took a couple of shots at me and obviously missed." She took my hand. It was time to work up more sympathy.

"They may try again," I said.

"Did you see who did it?" She was looking into my eyes, clearly concerned and interested.

"No, but I'd like it to stop. So I'm going to try to get some police protection for Judy and do my damndest to find out who killed Cash and is trying to make Judy and me a duo of death."

I'd heard that "duo of death" phrase in a *Captain Midnight* show and always wanted to work it into a conversation. This was the first chance I had. I pushed my hat back further on my head and took Cassie's hand in mind. I was glad she wasn't wearing her tape measure.

"I'll call the police and tell them what's happened. It might give them second thoughts about Wherthman being the killer. Then I'd better track down Clark Gable and check his version of what happened her yesterday morning."

"Is there anything I can do?" she asked. We were close enough together to exchange comments on our mouthwash, except I didn't use any. I hoped my dental sample smile lingered till noon. Hers did.

"Yes, there is," I said softly. "Find Hoff. Tell him that Cash was chummy with another midget, maybe even went into business with him. See if he can find out who it is. Wherthman is filling his time trying to come up with the name too. It may not be a lead, but it's worth a try."

She agreed and volunteered to do some checking on her own. She had worked on *Oz* for a short time and knew the names of a few of the midgets. I said thanks and lingered. She kissed me. It was a little more than motherly, but not enough to make anything out of.

"Be careful," she said, and I promised I would be.

She went off to look for Hoff and I picked up the phone. I didn't need to talk to Hoff right now, but I needed information and action. I called Andy Markopulis, the guy I knew who worked for M.G.M. security. He was at home building a patio with his kids. It was so wholesome I couldn't even make a joke about it. I explained the whole set-up to him and asked him to assign a couple of people to take off their uniforms and keep an eye on Judy Garland for a while. He said he'd assign two good men named Woodman and Fearaven. I didn't know them, but Andy knew his business.

Then I called my brother.

"Well?" he asked. "And if you ask me how Ruth and the kids are, I'll find you and punch your heart out."

"Someone tried to kill me and Judy Garland," I said.

"Bullshit."

"It's not bullshit," I said. "I've got bullet holes in my car windows."

"Bullshit," he repeated.

"For Chrissake, Phil, why would I lie?"

"It's an asshole stunt to get that little Nazi turd you're working for off the hook. Someone's trying to kill you and Garland. Wherthman's in the can, so it can't be him. That's the picture."

"So I shot bullet holes in my car windows?"

"Why not? That hunk of junk isn't worth ten dollars. It's about time you shot it and put it out of its misery. It reminds me of . . ."

71

"One of dad's old heaps," I finished. "Maybe that's why I like it."

He was quiet for a few seconds.

"How did they try to kill Garland?" he asked, but his voice showed he was humoring me.

"Poison," I said. "Someone left a water pitcher full of poison in her dressing room at the studio this morning. Someone noticed that it smelled funny."

"Where's the poison now?" he asked.

"They poured it out."

"That's a hell of a story, Tobias. Even if there was a pitcher of poison, which I doubt, you could have put it there, made sure she didn't drink it and then arranged for it to be conveniently dumped out before the police arrived. You've done worse."

He was right. I had done worse and was kind of proud of it, but this wasn't one of the times. I decided not to tell him about the phone calls to Garland and me from the unaccented man with the high voice. He wouldn't believe me.

"You're wrong, Phil."

"I've got a wave of ax murders waiting and no time for you. Now hang up and get a job as a night watchman."

"You're a whale, Phil," I sighed. "A goddamn whale with an eye on each side of your head. You try to juggle two separate images and miss what's right in front of you. Someday you're going to swim into an iceberg."

I hung up. Then I talked to the long distance operator and asked her to connect me to the William Randolph Hearst Ranch in San Simeon. I didn't have the number. I began to think I'd have to track down Hoff and get the number when I was connected to someone. It was a man who said, "Can I help you?"

I said he could if this was Bill Hearst's place, but I didn't say Bill and I didn't say place. I told him Clark Gable was expecting a call from me. He told me to wait, and there was some buzzing and clicking on the line. This time a woman's voice came on, and I repeated my message.

She said Mr. Gable and some other guests were on a picnic and wouldn't be back for three or four hours. I asked if someone could bring him a message and she said he was about ten miles away. Then she told me to wait. I waited, considering my next move. In a few minutes she came on.

"Mr. Gable left a message for you," she said. "If it's not inconvenient, you can come up here and see him this evening or call him tonight."

For a few good reasons, I decided to take the trip to San Simeon. First, I liked to be face to face with someone I'm talking to on a case. A facial expression or a move of the body might lead me somewhere. In addition, telephones demand action and business and hate silence. They don't give you much time to think, and I needed time to think. Going to San Simeon would give me some time and I had no other leads to follow. Getting out of town would also put distance between me and the guy who took the shots at me.

I drove off the lot, waving to Buck as I left, and checked my watch. It was almost noon. I beat the crowd to the Gotham Cafe on Hollywood and had an order of their special potato pancakes and sour cream to fortify myself for the trip. Then I was on my way.

In half an hour with the pistons churning, I shot

past Calabassas to the coast highway, and in a few minutes I was on El Camino Real, the Royal Highway. According to my Glendale high school days, the road along the ocean that stretched from San Diego to San Francisco was staked out in the 1780s or so by the Spanish. The Spanish were afraid the French or Russians would claim the land along the coast first. France had picked up a big chunk of land between the Mississippi and the Rocky Mountains. Russia was coming south across the Berring Sea and down the coast from what would eventually be Alaska.

The first big push to stake out the royal road stopped at what became Los Angeles. The whole point of the road was to set up a link between the Franciscan missions in California. The last long trek between Los Angeles and Monterey was done by a force of sixty-seven men under a Captain Portola and a Franciscan priest named Father Crespi.

I drove over the road at about 55 or 60, which was all out for the Buick, and wondered what Crespi and Portola would have thought about the gas stations, beaneries, writing on the rocks, and garbage. The missions were now tourist stops and the road paved with good intentions.

A long, dark cloud going as far as I could see along the coast and into the horizon kept me company for over 100 miles.

The car radio kept me company, too. I heard the news two or three times. The presidential campaign was over and everyone thought Willkie had taken the lead. Roosevelt said he was running because he could keep us out of the war. A writer named H. G. Wells had given a talk at the Ambassador Hotel in L.A. He wanted Americans to support Britain's war effort against the Germans.

From 1:30 to 3:30 in the afternoon I watched the scenery and listened to the Radio Parade for Roosevelt. Eleanor Roosevelt, Joseph P. Kennedy, Henry Fonda, Groucho Marx, Walter Huston, Katherine Hepburn, Lucille Ball, and Humphrey Bogart all told me why I should vote for F.D.R. Since I knew Bogart slightly, I was impressed, but I didn't think I was even registered to vote. I couldn't remember the last time I had voted. I was one hell of a good citizen.

I also found out that U.C.L.A. had been beaten by Stanford 20 to 14, and Minnesota had beaten Northwestern University 13 to 12. I didn't even know where Northwestern was.

It was dark when I hit San Simeon. I didn't see anything that looked like a big ranch or a road to it. I stopped at a gas station, filled up the Buick, and had a Pepsi. The guy at the station gave me directions to the Hearst place. I thanked him, took a bag of potato chips, and munched as I made my way, slowly looking for landmarks.

I pulled into what I thought was the right road, but I didn't see anything that looked like a ranch, just a little white house a few hundred yards up the road. A man stepped out of the little white house and held up his hand. He looked serious but not unfriendly. I could see another man through the window of the house watching me. Both men wore dark suits and black ties.

The man in the road walked over to the window of my car. I didn't have to roll down the window to talk because they were already down. I had driven drafty to hide the bullet holes. I could see that the guy, who looked something like a serious version of Buck Rogers, didn't think much of my transportation. I gave him a smile and offered him some potato chips. When he leaned over I could see that he was armed.

"Your name, sir?" he said politely.

"Toby Peters," I answered. He hadn't taken the chips so I put them back next to me.

He shouted to the other man in the house, giving my name, and the other guy shouted that I was expected.

I could see that the guy standing next to my car couldn't understand my invitation but he hid it well.

"O.K., sir, if you'll just follow this road slowly, you'll come to a place to park right near the big house," he said, pointing down the road.

"I don't see any house," I said.

"It's about five miles," he explained.

"You mean Hearst owns all this?" I asked.

"Just about as far as the eye can see in any direction on a clear day from the house. And the house is a few hundred feet up."

I was impressed.

"Now, sir," he went on, repeating something he had clearly gone through many times, "drive slowly with your lights on and give the right of way to any animals you meet."

"Animals?"

"Mr. Hearst has many wild animals on the property, including buffalo and zebras. The zebras are especially curious."

"I'll be careful," I said. I adjusted my tie and brushed potato chip crumbs from my lapels.

"One more thing," he added. "Please don't pick the

fruit. You'll find orange and apple trees near the house. They are never eaten."

I said I wouldn't eat the trees or kill the gorillas, and he held out his hand. It seemed silly to tip or shake, so I waited for an explanation.

"The hardware," he said.

I handed him the .38.

"We'll give it back when you leave. Be careful on the road. It twists upward. We'll give you twenty minutes to make it to the top. They'll let us know when you arrive. Don't stop, and don't get out of the car."

I went up the road with my lights on past the white house, where the other man watched me. The guy I had talked to stood in the road following my progress until I went out of sight around a curve more than 100 yards away.

A faint light glittered high above me out of the front of my window. It was to the right, and it looked very far. It might be the Hearst ranch.

I saw some kind of animal after two miles, but I couldn't make it out clearly. It was big and near the road. Bullet holes or not I rolled up the windows. My fears of a wild death were increasing. Now I could be eaten by an ape in Southern California.

When I got to the house, someone was there to meet me. He was built and dressed like the guys at the gate. They seemed to be a fraternity of former heavyweight champions. He motioned me to park and led me up a flight of stone steps and past nude statues. At the top of the steps we took a right and stopped in front of a huge house.

"Big place," I said.

"This is one of the guest houses," my guide said.

He knocked and went in. A group of people were sitting around a blazing fire in a big central room. One of them, a beautiful blonde who I should have recognized from some picture, said Gable was either in the big house or at the pool.

My guide led me out. We went into a courtyard and faced a building that looked like my dreams of a Gothic castle.

We went in, stepping over an inlaid tile floor and into a room as high as a cathedral. No one was in the room, which held tapestries on each wall. The tapestries, six of them, were more than twenty feet high and a few feet more than that across. There were lounges around the room and a lot of chairs, but no people.

A woman in a dark uniform appeared from nowhere, and my guide whispered to her and disappeared the way he had come. The woman motioned to me, and I followed her to a dark wood paneled wall which concealed a door.

"Is Baron Frankenstein home?" I asked her softly.

She didn't even acknowledge that I had spoken. We stepped into a high ceilinged room with cathedral-like windows and wooden church seats around the walls. A bunch of flags stuck out of the wall above. There was a long table stretching across the room with about thirty big, dark and ancient wooden chairs. We had walked out of Castle Frankenstein into a banquet set for The Crusades. Only one thing ruined the impression.

An old man in a dark suit sat at the center of the table. He had a hamburger in front of him and he was pouring a glob of Heinz ketchup on it. He didn't look up as we passed.

"Servants get to use the main room before supper?" I whispered to the hurrying lady in front of me.

"That," she said, "was Mr. Hearst. He's having a snack before the main meal."

I tried to turn back and get a look at the old man, but the woman was hurrying along in front of me. I never got a look at her face. We went outside, down a path, and then into a building.

It was the fanciest damn indoor pool I've ever seen. It must have been forty yards long and tiled from ceiling to pool bottom. The place radiated blue and was pleasantly warm. A few people were in the water. One of them inched his way toward me and pulled himself out of the pool.

It was Clark Gable. He picked up a towel and dried his hands as he stepped forward and smiled. He took my hand.

"Toby Peters, isn't it? Good to meet you."

"Good to meet you," I said. He went to a bench against the wall, and I followed him as he continued to dry himself.

"Want to take a swim before we talk?" he asked. I said I didn't swim.

"I don't either," he said, running the towel over his hair. "Not more than a few strokes. And this damn pool is over my head. There's no shallow end. There's an outdoor pool with a shallow end on the other side of the house, but it's too cold tonight to go out."

I tried to look sympathetic, and he gave me a wry smile I recognized. It was his Academy Award smile.

"You don't think much of all this, do you, Peters?" he said, indicating that he meant the whole Hearst set-up.

"Does it matter?" I said.

"Sure," he said, working on his feet.

"I'm impressed," I said. "I'm a two-buck private investigator with two suits and a one-room shack in Los Angeles. This man could buy a whole damn city."

"Maybe more," Gable added. "This is probably the most expensive toy anyone ever had. It's filled with enough to stock ten museums. Hearst is a collector, of things and people."

"And you're one of them?" I asked.

"No," he laughed. "Mostly, I'm a friend of a friend of Mr. Hearst. I've done some work with Marion Davies. She invited me up for the weekend. As rich as Mr. Hearst is, I don't think he could afford me. He could have a few years ago, though. Now, would you like a drink, or do you want to talk here? I'm through here, and I'll be getting dressed for dinner in a little while."

I said I'd talk here. I tried not to watch the people diving in the pool from what looked like a marble balcony.

"Shoot," said Gable with a wave of his hand.

"You saw two midgets arguing at the studio?"

"Right." He said looking at me the way he looked at Thomas Mitchell in *Gone With the Wind*. "One of them is dead—murdered, I hear."

"Yes. Did the police talk to you about that?"

"For a few minutes on the phone. I was on my way up here. They said they could get the details from Vic Fleming and another witness."

"Did you see that other witness?" I asked. "A big, muscular guy?"

"Nope," said Gable. "Just the two little fellas going

at it. Vic wanted to hurry on so we didn't see very much."

"Describe what you did see."

He described the costumes of the two little men and added that he and Fleming had been too far away to hear their words or tell me if either of them had an accent. "I do remember that the shorter of the two seemed to be getting the worst of it from the one in the uniform," said Gable.

Gunther Wherthman had said one of the reasons Cash had hated him was that he was bigger than Cash. Now Gable was telling me that Cash was taller than the man he was arguing with.

"Wait, are you sure the Munchkin in uniform—the one with the feather in his hat and the yellow beard—was taller than the other one?" I asked slowly. "You said you weren't very close."

"He was taller," said Gable confidently. "I may not be a great judge of character, but I'll put money on my judgment of perspective."

"You'd testify to that?" I asked.

"If it came to it," he said. "Is it important?"

"You may have just saved the life of one tiny Swiss translator."

"Glad to do it," he beamed. "Say, how'd you like to stay for dinner and the movie? There's a movie here every night in the theater."

"He has a theater, too?" My eyes wandered around the pool house again, and to the beautiful swimmers in the water. I was definitely out of my league. "Thanks just the same," I said, standing up, "but I've got to head back to L.A."

He stood with me, shook my hand, and patted me on the back.

"Happy I could help, Peters," he said. The towel was around his neck and he was gripping it in both hands. His dark hair fell over his brow. All he needed was Victor Fleming and a camera crew.

The uniformed woman without a face led me around the house instead of through it and back to the man who had met me at my car. She turned and walked away.

"Nice meeting you!" I shouted. The man in the dark suit took me right to my car door and tucked me in. He made no comment on the bullet holes. I said good-bye and drove down the road. It was dark and the sky was star-filled when I reached the gate and the two men who manned it. One stepped out and handed me my .38. I said thanks and he said, "You're welcome, sir."

I headed back south for an hour or so and decided to stop at a diner. After I ate the spaghetti special, coffee and pie, I drove to a motor court to register. It reminded me of a clean version of my own place. It was called Happy Byways Motor Court, and Mrs. Happy Byways took my two bucks, gave me a receipt, and handed me the key to Bungalow Six, recently painted white. She was too fat to move and was covered with what looked like a blanket. I thanked her and went to Six after she sold me the Sunday *L.A. Times.*

The radio in the room didn't work so I read the paper. King Doob was missing and Buck Rogers had to find him. Something was missing for me, too, but I didn't know what it was. I decided to sleep on it. I had no razor or toothpaste so I just showered and went to bed. Happy Byways seemed safe enough, but I put my gun under my pillow just in case and propped a chair in front of the door. I felt confident enough to leave the light out in the bathroom. I think that confidence saved my life.

Before I went to sleep I felt my stomach to see if it was losing tone. I hadn't hit the Y for days. My stomach seemed all right, so I closed my eyes and was out.

I dreamed of midgets crawling in under the cracks and through the drains. They oozed through a chimney and went for me with long, thin knives. I fought to wake up and heard a sound at the door, but I was too befuddled to respond. The chair in front of the door slowed my guest down, but just a little. The door broke, the chair flew, and he stood framed against the faint light. The form in the door was no midget. The bed wasn't in line with the door so I was in darkness. With the bathroom light off he had to take a guess. The guess was good. He hit the bed and one bullet thudded into the wall over my head. I fumbled for my .38 and fired. I wasn't even worried about hitting him. I just wanted him to know I was armed. For all I know, my bullet hit the ceiling.

The figure in the doorway backed out fast, and I got out of bed in shorts and ran after him. I fell over the chair that had been propped in front of the door. By the time I got outside, I could see a car pulling into the highway, but I couldn't be sure of the color, and I couldn't make out anything on the license.

It was a big, newish car, and I had no chance of catching him. Even if I did want to take a chance, I was standing in my shorts, holding a gun, and people were popping their heads out of the windows of the court around me.

"It's all right!" I shouted. "I'm the police."

I walked back into my room slowly and closed the door. My explanation would hold them for about five minutes. I dressed in two and went to the Happy Byways office. The fat woman wasn't there, but the light was on. The clock on the wall said 2 A.M. I reached for the registration book as I heard her grunting to her feet in the next room. I tore out the page with my name on it, jammed it in my pocket, and went out the door before she took a step. I didn't want to do any explaining.

I drove for about fifty miles, trying to think straight. The impression had been brief, but I had seen a big figure in that door. When I was certain that no one was in sight, I pulled behind a hill on my right and turned off my lights. I had an old picnic blanket in the trunk. I got it out and climbed in the back seat after reloading the .38. I fell asleep in a few minutes, clutching my gun like a cold teddy bear.

5

WINTER IS THE mischief in me. I heard a scratching sound and sat upright in the back seat. Something was at the front window. I shot. The window shattered and I missed the collie by about a foot. I heard him trotting away and barking in fear. I knew how he felt.

I sat upright and discovered another problem. Sea dampness, dew, and a contorted position for six hours had done in my back. The injury went back to a black guy who didn't like my kidneys and had told them so. When wet weather hit, I felt as if my vertebrae were welded together, surrounded by a sensitive band of exposed nerves.

The groaning helped a little as I rolled on my side and went through the door. The collie stood on a hill watching. In about two minutes he saw me make it into the front seat and brush away the glass. I had nothing to kill the pain, but I knew someone who did. I got into a position I could barely live with, tucked the .38 into my holster, cursed the ocean which I could see a few hundred feet below me, and got back on the highway.

Part of the drive back wasn't bad. I mean I wasn't in total burning agony. I got hungry in an hour, but I didn't want to get out of the car. I wasn't sure I could. Just before noon, I found a place near Santa Barbara where you could honk your horn for service. I honked my horn at the El Camino Drive-In, and a skinny, red-headed girl in a tacky red uniform approached me. She stopped when she looked at my stubble-covered and anguish-filled face.

"You all right?" she said.

"Wife just had a baby," I explained. "Been up all night."

"Congratulations," she said with an accent out of Missouri or Oklahoma. "Boy or girl?"

"Girl. Eleanor Roosevelt Peters."

She took my groaned order: two egg sandwiches with mayonaise and a chocolate shake.

When I finished eating, I pulled a buck out of my pocket, but Missouri wouldn't take it.

"Boss says it's on the house. For the new daddy."

Her smile was crooked and nice, and I felt like an Italian in Ethiopia. I smiled back and left.

Some time late in the afternoon I pulled in front of the Farraday Building into a no parking zone. The next trick was to get out of the car. While I was trying, Jeremy Butler stepped out for some Lysol-free air and saw me.

"You get shot again?" he asked, taking my arm.

"No, it's my back. Can you help me up to the office?"

Butler picked me up as if I were helium-filled and walked me into the building.

"I've known lots of guys with bad backs," he said, going up the stairs instead of taking the elevator. I weighed a solid 165 pounds and it was dead weight, but he didn't seem to notice.

"Know any body builders?" I asked.

"Some," he said, moving steadily upward. "Different muscles from wrestlers. They're top-heavy. No center of gravity."

The pain was still there, but I could tell Butler was doing his best to be gentle.

"I mean personalities," I said.

"All kinds," Butler said. "Some fairies, some skirt chasers. A few momma's boys. All exhibitionists. They want people to look at them. Someone. A mother, father, someone didn't pay attention, and they're making up for it. Some of them are good guys."

"You're a poet, Jer," I said as he elbowed his way into the alcove of Minck and Peters. The alcove was barely big enough for both of us. He hurried through. Shelly was eating a sweet roll and smoking a cigar while he read a Western in his dental chair. Butler told him to get up, and he deposited me carefully in the seat of honor. I groaned once for sympathy. Butler wasn't even breathing hard.

"Get shot?" Shelly asked with more curiosity than sympathy.

"No, buddy," I said through my teeth. "It's my back. You got something to kill the pain?"

"Sure," he said, and went for the needle. "I'll give you a shot and some pills, but you're better off going to bed for a few days and letting it take care of itself."

"I may not have a few days," I said. Shelly rolled up my shirt and gave me a shot in the lower back.

"I use it on gums," he said to Butler, "but it's supposed to work anywhere."

He gave me an unmarked bottle with about ten pills in it. I took one out and swallowed it, gasping for water. Shelly turned on his dental chair water, and I drank out of the dirty glass cup. I curled over in agony waiting for the shot and the pill to do their stuff. While I waited, I told Shelly and the landlord about Judy Garland, the dead Munchkin, and the two attempts on my life. Shelly had heard part of it before, but he had been so busy saving the tooth of Walter Brennan's double that he had forgotten.

"Let me try something," Butler said, picking me up. I didn't want to be picked up; the dental pain killers hadn't done their stuff yet. But I was in no condition to argue. Butler put me on the floor and rolled me on my stomach. I didn't go completely over because I was in an almost fetal position. He put his left hand on my spine and his fingers over my kidney. He grabbed my collar bone at the top of my back. The push down and pull up was sudden and without warning. There was a sound like an inner tube snapping, and a rush of pain.

"There," said Butler. "How do you feel?"

I started to roll back into my protected fetal position and realized that the bad pain was gone. My lower back still felt sore, but it was tolerable.

I got up a little shaky, but I knew I could walk and feel something besides pain.

"Shot's working," explained Shelly, pointing his cigar at me with professional pride. "Take those pills and you'll be fine for a day or so."

Butler said nothing. He just looked tolerantly at Shelly with tiny blue eyes.

"Thanks," I said to both of them, and hobbled into my office. There was almost no pain when I got to my desk and picked up the phone. I could hear the door open and Butler leave. Shelly began to hum "Take Me Out to the Ball Game" off-key, and I asked the operator for M.G.M. Hoff wasn't there. I called his home number. He answered.

"Hoff, did Cassie tell you about the other midget, the one Wherthman says was chummy with Cash?"

"It's Sunday," he said in apology. "I can't reach anyone, but I'm sure I'll know by tomorrow."

"Today would be nice," I said. "Work on it. Who's Wherthman's lawyer?"

"A guy named Leib, Marty Leib. His office is on . . ."

"I need his home number," I said. "I may not have until tomorrow. Is he listed?"

Hoff didn't know, but he had the home number written down. He was a good leg man.

"One last thing, Hoff. Where were you late last night?"

"Why?" he asked.

"Someone about your size took a shot at me in a motor court up the coast."

"Why the hell would I want to kill you?" he shouted. The anger sounded real, but I'd seen him change personalities almost in mid-sentence.

"Where were you?" I demanded.

"Here. Right here all night."

"You've got a witness?" I pushed.

"My wife," he said pulling himself together. I could see his hand touching his hair into place. I wondered if he was wearing a purple velvet robe and slippers and holding a copy of the *New Yorker* in his hand.

"Wives have lied for husbands," I said.

He didn't answer.

"You there, Warren?"

"I'm here. You need anything else?"

"You owe me another day's pay and expenses. I'll send you the bill," I said, and waited for him to hang up. We played "you first" for about twenty seconds and I hung up.

I called lawyer Leib, whose bass voice almost knocked me off the chair.

"Ah, Mr. Peters!" he boomed. "I wanted to get in touch with you. Our client has a message for you. The name of the other midget, Cash's friend. It's John Franklin Peese."

I asked him to spell it while I fished around for my gnawed pencil and an envelope to write on. I found the envelope addressed to me by Merle Levine, the lady whose cat I never found.

"I'll work on it," I said, and I told him about Clark Gable's confidence that the arguing suspect was shorter than the victim.

Leib said that was great, but he was hoping Peese would lead to something better. He wanted to avoid a trial and publicity. Having Clark Gable as the key witness for the defense in what looked like an open-and-shut case wouldn't do anyone any good. Leib said I should call him at any time, and we hung up good pals.

The next trick was to find John Franklin Peese, but first I called Andy Markopulis. He told me Woodman and Fearaven were at Judy Garland's house and nothing had happened. Records of present and former employees were at the studio, and Peese would surely be listed. Andy said he could meet me at the studio if I wished. I said I'd think about it and call him back.

While I was thinking about it, Cassie James called.

She said she wanted to know how the talk with Gable had gone and how I was. I told her about it and the attempt on my life. I had liked the way she moved toward me the last time I was almost done in. Her voice did it over the phone. Then she told me she knew the name of the midget Gunther Wherthman was trying to think of. She gave me Peese's name, and said she could get into the personnel records and get an address. That sounded like more fun than meeting Andy Markopulis and I asked where she'd be. She said at home, and invited me over for dinner. I accepted, and she gave me a Santa Monica address and a couple of hours to get to it.

The pain in my back was almost gone. I decided to take a chance on going home for a shave and bath. An hour later I was shaved and clean, and my teeth weren't furry anymore. I gulped one of Shelly's pain pills just in case and went out the door into the evening sun looking for an unfriendly face attached to a big body. None appeared.

The drive was uneventful. No one tried to kill me, and it was a dead Sunday. Paper blew in the streets. Mexicans with nothing to do sat on the curbs arguing. Anglos with lawns cut the grass.

KMPC radio said they'd broadcast a "Hollywood on Parade" for Willkie the next day with Conrad Nagel, Edward Arnold, Porter Hall and Arthur Lake. Roosevelt had the clear edge in star power. I turned off the radio and headed for Cassie James.

Her house was on the beach in Santa Monica. It wasn't a big money place, but it wasn't welfare living, either. I didn't know exactly what her job at M.G.M. was or how much she was paid. My estimate jumped when I got out of the car. She had some money.

The surf rolled in and grumbled, and the sun was cut off halfway on the horizon. She answered the door with a small smile, and I figured out her color code. Today she was wearing a yellow blouse and skirt. She was a woman of solid colors. No stripes, designs or little flowers. It made her seem solid. The house matched. None of the furniture in the living room had a stripe or flower. Even the paintings on the white walls weren't flowery. She caught me looking at the room instead of at her.

"What do you think?"

"It's restful," I said, putting my hat on a table near the door and dropping into a sofa to rest. There was plenty of room on the sofa for company. She sat next to me and handed me a card. Neatly written on it in green ink was the name of James Franklin Peese and an address on Main Street. I tucked it in my pocket, and Cassie James moved closer to me.

"Hungry?" she said.

"Always," I answered, which was nearly the truth.

I could feel her breath on me and looked into her eyes.

"Let's skip the game," she said softly. "I've played it a few times. It's embarrasing, awkward, and it makes me feel foolish."

She got up and led me into a bedroom. The room was painted yellow. The bed and furniture were black.

"We'll eat later," she said. "It'll be easier for both of us."

She held out her hand for my coat, and I gave it to her. Then she turned her hand down, palm up, toward my pants and left the room turning down the lights. I took my clothes off, put them on a chair, and got into

MURDER ON THE YELLOW BRICK ROAD

the bed. I worked over a couple of wise cracks in my head in case she came back in an apron with a tray of chicken. She came back without chicken, and I made no cracks. She was dark and beautiful, and came to me softly smelling of mountains. I dropped back with her on top of me. We didn't talk and moved slowly. It was better than I had imagined, and the sound of the sea outside helped.

I almost fell asleep, but not quite, and she kissed me awake.

"Hungry?"

I said yes, and she got up, slowly throwing her hair back, and went toward the living room. I closed my eyes for a few minutes or half an hour.

She came back dressed in a black knit sweater and skirt.

"You've got five minutes," she whispered.

I grunted and got up when she left. In a few minutes I was dressed. Before I went into the living room, I took another one of Shelly's just-in-case pain pills and gulped it down with tap water in Cassie's pink bathroom. There was better behavior for a bad back than what I was doing.

We had dinner in a corner of the living room next to a window where we could see the moon and the coast. We ate steak and corn on the cob, and there was plenty of it. We both had a beer and talked about nothing.

"Ever married?" I said, when we had put the dishes away.

"Once, for a short time, a long time ago. You?"

"Once," I said, "for a long time, until a short time ago."

There didn't seem much else to say on the subject. We talked about Judy Garland. I told my life story, making myself look as tough as possible. She gave me a little about her life, but not much more than she had before. We talked about Hoff and made jokes about his first-naming and changes in personality, and I told her about my meeting with Mayer. She had never talked to Mayer, nor been in his office in the years; she had worked in the studio. She'd begun with M.G.M. shortly after she had come from Texas. Her career as an actress had passed after a few years, and she had devoted herself to her actress sister. When the sister died, Cassie had plunged into costume design and had done well as an assistant. She didn't talk about men, but I was sure she would have if I'd asked.

Somewhere after eleven she said she had to get to bed alone because she had to be at the studio at six. We kissed and I started to prolong it, but she pushed me away gently with the promise of more in the future.

"I'll talk to you tomorrow," I said.

"I'll be waiting," she said, and I strode out to my Buick as if it were an armed charger.

When I got back home I felt confident about killing any dragons that might want to break into my castle. Besides, the dragon who was trying to kill me was a lousy shot. I was confident, but not stupid. I put my sofa in front of the door, kept the bathroom light out, and put the gun under my pillow. My back felt great.

I dreamed Roosevelt was campaigning in Munchkinland, promising to keep wicked witches out. A couple of Munchkins with long knives crept up behind him as he talked. The other Munchkins and Glinda, the good witch, saw the tiny killers but said nothing. It was up to me to save the President. I tried to run forward, but my back was too sore. I tried to shout, but nothing came out. I watched in helpless horror. Glinda, looking very much like Cassie and dressed in solid red, took me in her arms and comforted me. It felt good, and I felt guilty as hell.

6

S CREW Chiquita Banana. I always kept my bananas in the refrigerator. They turned brown and looked like hell, but they lasted longer. I found one survivor behind a jar of grape jelly. Ignoring the color, I sliced it into little pieces and sprinkled it on top of my bowl of Wheaties. Then sugar and milk. Top with a cup of Hill's or Chase and Sanborn, and you have the Peters gourmet breakfast, which is just what I had that Monday morning while I read the newspaper. The previous tenant hadn't cancelled his subscription, and once in a while I got up early enough to grab the paper before a neighbor stole it. Today was such a day. I put my back to the wall of my little alcove kitchen, placed my .38 on the table in front of me, and read while I ate.

An eight-column headline said the presidential election would be the closest since 1916. I tried to figure out who had run in 1916. It was too late for Lincoln and too early for Hoover. Gallup indicated that the Willkie trend was running strong.

With a fresh shirt on my back, a relatively clean tie around my neck, memories of Cassie James in my mind, another day's pay coming from M.G.M., a back free from pain, and hope in my future, I stepped out of my door and into a puddle of mud. I fell on my ass. I had slept through a late season rain during the night.

A change of clothes put a new suit on my back and a wary look in my eye when I stepped out of the same door ten minutes later. The gods had warned me not to be such a smart ass about the future, and I read the warning.

John Franklin Peese's address on Main near Jefferson was a long walk from my place, but it could be walked. I drove and made it in less than ten minutes. It was one of those typically dingy neighborhoods that surround most downtown areas of big cities. I knew the area well; my office was a few blocks away. I parked in a garage on Broadway and walked back. Normally, I would have parked on the street, but with no windows that was asking for a stripped or missing car in this neighborhood.

Main was a busy downtown street, one of the busiest, with fat buildings and restaurants. In this area there were nickel hot dog stands and flop houses.

I stopped in front of 134 Main. It was a flop. The sign read: BEDS 15 CENTS, ROOMS 35 CENTS, HOT AND COLD WATER. Next door to the flop was a nickel movie house which boasted all seats for five cents. "Big Show. Little Price." One sign said there were five pictures. Another sign said there were six. A poster showed Tom Tyler with a gun in his right hand and a girl in his left looking up at him. Tom was all in black and the picture was *The Feud of the Trail*. The nickel show also promised the first chapter of a Ken Maynard Western, *Mystery Moun-*

tain. A guy in a milkman's suit with a thin jacket over it tilted his white cap back and studied the posters. I stood next to him wondering who it would hurt if I spent the day in the dark.

The milkman went in, but I didn't follow him. I went into the flop house. It took about thirty seconds to adjust from the light to the dusty darkness of a lobby of forty-watt bulbs.

The forty-watters were a good idea. They saved the management money, and they made it hard to see the lobby. The lobby was small and decorated in early 20th century junk. It was the kind of place in which Shelly Minck picked up most of his trade, and his trade picked up most of its diseases.

When my eyes adjusted to the dim yellow light, I went to the desk. I passed a guy sitting in one of the two lounge chairs in the lobby. I didn't give him a second look, but I held him in mind. He was too damn well-dressed to be sitting around in the morning in a place like this. It was a warm day, and the parks were free. On a day like this even a bum knew enough to hike the few blocks to Exposition Park.

The guy behind the desk was wearing a ratty sweater and a jacket. His nose was running. He had a cold, and I didn't want to get too near him. It might not be a cold. He was bald with big freckles on his scalp. His chest was caved in as if he had taken one big cough and had never recovered. His belly flowed out and he could have been any age for 25 to 50.

"My name's Peters," I said quietly and seriously. "I'm involved in an investigation, and I'd like to have some information on one of your tenants."

He blew his nose on a dirty handkerchief, pushed

the handkerchief into his trouser pocket, and looked at me with moist eyes.

"Mr . . . ?" I tried again.

"Valentine," he said. "I only use one name."

"Like Garbo," I said.

"She's got another name," he said. "I only use the one."

"You in show business?" I said.

"No," he sneered. "Who you want to know about?"

"Peese," I said. "John Franklin Peese."

"Don't recall him," said Valentine, retrieving his handkerchief.

"You can't miss him," I said softly, overcoming my repulsion and leaning toward him. "He's only about three feet tall."

Valentine gave a good blow and seemed to be thinking about people three feet tall.

"Who's the night man?" I asked.

"I am," he said. "I don't leave here. Sleep back there." He pointed to a door behind him.

"Look in your book," I said wearily.

"You ain't a cop," he said, turning away.

"Three bucks," I said.

"Five," he said.

"Good-bye," I said.

"Wait," he said.

We both knew how the conversation would go, but the rules of conduct made us ride out the race. I'd played it dozens of times, and I knew it wasn't over. I counted out three bucks and he said, "Room 31."

I started to turn and he added, "But he's not there anymore. Moved out about five months ago. Glad to see him go. He was a mean little fart."

"You got an address for him," I said, keeping my back to the counter. The well-dressed man in the lobby was pretending to read a book, but I knew he could hear what we said.

"He didn't leave one," said Valentine, purring.

"You have some idea of where I can find him?" I said.

He took too long to answer "no," so I knew he had something, maybe just a badly congested nose, but I took a chance. I didn't want to do it, but I couldn't horse around here all day playing games. I turned slowly, pulled two bucks out of my wallet and reached over the counter grabbing Valentine by the sweater. Part of it came off in my hands. I grabbed again and pulled him into the counter. Our faces were inches apart. He smelled like Friday's garbage on Monday morning. I thought both of us were about to throw up. Him in fear; me in disgust.

"I heard he was someplace downtown," he squeaked.

"Where?" I asked with a forced smile.

"I don't know, one of the big hotels," Valentine said, gasping for air. "One of the guys who flops here saw him. He said Peese looked like he'd made the big time. Big cigar. The works. Peese wouldn't give him the price of a small flop. He's a bastard, that little one, a bastard."

I let him down gently. His sweater was bunched up on his bird chest, and he was panting. I must have looked to him like my brother looks to me.

"Sorry about that," I said. "This'll buy you another sweater and a last name." I dropped five more on the counter. He could get ten sweaters for less than that within a block.

"I don't want a last name," he said, putting the five

under the counter. "What good's a last name done any-body?"

He had a point.

I walked into the sun, and my eyes closed. I waited until I was out of sight of the door before I wiped my hands of Valentine's grime. I knew a shortcut back to Broadway through an alley. I'd chased a kid through it once when I was doing a month as a bouncer at the Broadway Bar in '37. Since most of the customers were bar flies and winos, I'd built up a good win-loss record. But the two or three good losses were enough to make me go back to my private investigating, Depression or no Depression. One of the losses had left me with my scalp split like a car seat that spent too much time in the desert.

The happy memory faded as I stepped into the alley and realized two things. First, I had to look forward to a day of looking for a midget in downtown hotels. He might not even be in a downtown hotel. Valentine might have got the word wrong, or the bum who passed it might have messed it up or dreamed it, but I had to give it a try. Most of my investigating involved following leads that lead nowhere. The cops did the same thing, but there were lots of cops.

The second thing I realized was that someone was following me. I didn't want to turn back. If it was the dragon with the bad shot, he might shoot sooner than he planned if I turned. I kept walking through the alley around garbage cans, looking for an open door and ex-pecting a bullet in the back. I had taken one there not too long ago. I didn't want to press my luck. Even the bat who was trying to do me in would have the odds going for him eventually.

He didn't know how to tail, and I could see his long shadow out of the corner of my eye as it hit the brick wall. He was hurrying now to keep up, but I didn't want to break. My armpits were damp, and Broadway was just a dozen yards or so ahead. I made up my mind, reached for my gun as I walked and took a sudden turn into a doorway.

The guy behind me stumbled forward, and I moved out with my .38 under his nose and grabbed a hunk of his jacket. It was the well-dressed guy in the flop house lobby. I pulled him into the doorway and pushed him into shadow. He looked surprised, but only a little and not at all scared. I felt him for a weapon the way the Glendale cops had taught me a tenth of a century earlier. He came away clean, and I looked at him. He wore a light grey suit with a white tie and shirt. He wasn't dressed for tailing. He stood out like a snowball in a coal pile.

He was in his fifties. His face was round, and his mouth was small and a little weak. His nose was straight, and he wore round tortoise glasses. His hairline was falling back and his hair was thin, but he had it combed forward on the left to battle the receding glacier of time.

"O.K.," I said. "Who are you, and why are you following me?"

He took out a pipe and lit it. His hands weren't shaking and his voice was a little high, but perfectly calm.

"My name's Chandler, Raymond Chandler," he said, getting the pipe going. "I'm a writer. I write detective stories and novels."

"That doesn't explain why you were in the lobby of that bedbug palace and why you followed me," I whispered through my teeth. It was my best shot at menace, but he looked interested and amused.

"I often sit around hotel lobbies picking up characters and dialogue," he explained. "That is a little lower than the places I usually sit around in, but it was worth it. I found you. You're the first real private investigator I've seen at work."

I couldn't tell if he was putting on an act or if he was what he said. His story sounded dumb.

"What books have you written?" I said. I put my gun back in my holster, but I didn't lean back.

"Well," he said. "I did one called *The Big Sleep* and a few months ago another one of mine, *Farewell, My Lovely*, came out."

I'd never heard of him or them, and I said so.

"The number of mystery novels that have had even minimal success in the past five years can be counted on one hand of a two-toed sloth," he sighed.

It sounded like writer talk.

"You don't look dangerous to me," I admitted, "but . . ."

"I'm a pretty dangerous man with a wet towel," he grinned. "But my favorite weapon is a twenty-dollar bill when I have one, which is seldom. Look, you can check on me easily enough. My publisher is Knopf. I'll give you a number to call, or you can look it up yourself. I live at 449 San Vincente Boulevard in Santa Monica with my wife Cissy. You can call her up."

I told him I'd do just that and guided him onto Broadway and into a tavern. The phone was on the wall, and I had Chandler stand where I could see him. I had the impression that he was usually a sad man with a world-weary look, but something had awakened him, and he was smiling as he smoked.

I called an L.A. number Chandler gave me. It was a literary agency. I checked it in the phone book as I talked. I asked the guy if he had heard of Chandler, and he said he had. I asked for a description, and he gave me a pretty good one. I hung up.

"You're a careful man, Mr. . . ."

"Peters," I said. "Toby Peters. I make up in caution what I lack in brains."

"Can I buy you lunch or a beer, Mr. Peters?" Chandler said.

In ten minutes, I had pushed around a warped desk clerk and a well-meaning solid citizen. I had worked up an appetite. We found a place on the block where steak sandwiches could be had with beer and I could sit with my back to the wall watching the door. Chandler might not be the only one following me. I told Chandler my tale, and he listened. I think for a minute he decided I was nuts, but I offered to let him call Warren Hoff at Metro. He declined.

"I probably make up in brains what I lack in caution," he said. "Peters. I have an offer for you. I heard what happened at that flop house. You're going to start looking for that midget, right?"

I said I was.

"Good," he said. "I'll help you if you like. It'll be good background material, and it will help make up for my giving you a scare."

It would also cheer up a man who needed cheering, and I meant Chandler, not me. I could use the help even if he didn't give me much, and he was good company.

"Fine," I said. "Pay the bill, and let's get going."

We drove the few blocks to my office, and Chandler turned his head to soak in the smell of Lysol and the atmosphere. I introduced him to Shelly, who was working on a regular customer, a kid who looked like Alfalfa in Our Gang. Shelly was trying to straighten the kid's teeth or kill him in the attempt.

I told Shelly that Chandler wrote detective stories, but Shelly had never heard of him.

"You got an overbite problem there, Ray," Shelly said, pointing his cigar at Chandler and looking over the top of his thick glasses. "I'll take a look when I finish with my friend here."

"Some other time," said Chandler with a smile.

"Suit yourself," shrugged Shelly, making it clear the loss was Chandler's. The kid in the chair was sitting with his mouth wide open. I motioned to him to close it. Shelly breathed on his mirror and wiped it clear on his dirty coat before turning to the kid, whose mouth flew open as if it were hinged.

"Landlord's a writer," said Shelly probing the kid's mouth. "Writes poetry. You should meet him. He used to be a wrestler."

"I used to think I was a poet," said Chandler. The sad look started to cloud his face, and I hustled him into my office.

I picked up the phone and asked the operator if there was a directory listing for John Franklin Peese. She said there wasn't which didn't surprise me. There were a few ways to try to track down Peese. I could try theatrical agents in the hope that he was in entertainment, but it was a longshot. I could also ask my brother to see if Cash, the dead midget, had an address or number for Peese in his effects. If they knew each other, it was possible. But I doubted if Phil would give me the information.

I pulled out a phone book, sat Chandler at my desk, and told him to start at the A's and call downtown hotels. I'd go back from the Z's. When we hit the M's, if we did before we got a lead, we'd talk it over. I told him we'd consider Downtown as a rectangle bordered by Alpine, Seventh, Figueroa, and Alameda. If we didn't hit anything in that square we'd consider spreading it out or giving up on the idea.

"If they ask, say you're the police," I said. "If they want your name, make one up, but remember what it is. If they say they have no one named Peese, then say you're a cop even if they don't ask and find out if they have any midgets registered."

He nodded and plunged eagerly into the book while I went out. I could hear him saying, "Alexandria Hotel?" when I closed the door. It might turn out to be one hell of a phone bill, but M.G.M. would pay it if I had to itemize every hotel called. There was a pay phone in the hall, and I left Shelly humming when I went to it with a pocketful of nickels.

Two of the first five hotels I called thought I was pulling some midget gag.

About fifteen minutes later, when I was about to give the operator the number of the Natick Hotel, Chandler hurried into the hall, looking both ways.

"Got it!" he yelled. I hung up and moved to his side.

The hotel was a big one downtown. Peese was registered under his own name and was in his room. Chandler had not asked to speak to him. He had thought fast and said he wanted to mail something to Peese and was confirming his address.

We got in the Buick, cut across the Figueroa, and went the few blocks downtown. While we drove, I told him about a case I'd been on in which I'd spent two weeks looking for a runaway husband who turned out to be hiding in a crawlspace in his own basement. Chandler smoked, listened and said more to himself than me, "Funny thing, civilization. It promises so much, and what it delivers is mass production of shoddy merchandise and shoddy people."

There wasn't time for much more conversation, and I had the feeling that a full day's talk with Chandler in his present mood would send me running for the night watchman's job my brother wanted me to take.

I found a space on the street, and we walked to the hotel. It had a doorman who recognized Chandler as a potential customer and accepted me as a character. I told Chandler to let me do the talking, and we crossed to the desk. There were two clerks, and one stepped forward with a slight smile.

"Yes?" he said.

"John Franklin Peese," I said. "His room, please."

The clerk looked at me and Chandler.

"I'll announce you," he said, and I put up a hand to stop him.

"Mr. Peese is my brother," I said. "I haven't seen him in years. I'd like to surprise him."

The clerk looked suspicious and Chandler said, "Mr. Peese's condition is not hereditary. He is the only one of four brothers who is a midget."

The clerk waivered, but hesitated. We had him on the brink, and I didn't want Peese to duck on us.

"I don't know," he said. He had a little mustache that looked painted on. He played with it. "Mr. Peese has . . ."

"A temper," I finished, faking anger, "and that is inherited in our family."

I had purposely raised my voice and Chandler took the cue. He stepped forward and pretended to calm me.

"All right," said the clerk recognizing the familial temperament if not the face and body. "He's in 909."

"Thank you," Chandler said while I stalked toward the elevators.

"Wait down here," I whispered to Chandler. "Go back and apologize to the clerk for my shouting. Keep him from calling Peese as long as you can." Chandler nodded and hurried back to the desk clerk, who was watching me. I glared at him while I waited for the elevator. When it came, Chandler was nodding in sympathy to something the clerk had said.

On the elevator, I had a few seconds to consider my approach to Peese. I could make up a story, say I was an agent or theater owner or producer and get him talking, but it might be awkward to work the conversation around to the murder. I could pretend I was a cop or at least give the impression, but if Peese was the kind of character Wherthman and Valentine said he was, he might complain and get my license pulled.

When the elevator groaned to a stop at nine, I decided to hit him with something close to the truth. He might just get mad enough to say something. I couldn't picture myself muscling a midget, but I might be able to do it. Maybe I could push him to get me mad enough.

I trotted down the hall to 909. Chandler seemed to be doing the job I gave him, but I didn't know how long he could hold the clerk. I was knocking loud at 909 when I heard the phone ring inside.

"Who is it?" asked a high, petulant voice.

"My name's Peters," I said. "I'm a private detective, and I want to talk to you."

The phone kept ringing.

"About what?" said the voice.

My name didn't seem to mean anything to him, which implied that he didn't know anything about who was trying to kill me, and that he probably wasn't the one who made the call to Shelly about my address.

"Murder," I said. "The murder of a little man named Cash."

"Screw off," he screeched. The phone kept ringing.

"Right," I said. "I'll just go the lobby and call the cops. I work for M.G.M., and my job is to keep things quiet, but if you want noise, you'll find out what noise is when the cops get here and start asking things like where were you Friday morning? How well did you know Cash? What business were the two of you in? Why have so many people talked about the fights you had with him?"

The phone stopped ringing. He had answered it. I put my ear to the door and heard venom spit from his mouth as he said, "Thanks, you mental cripple. He's here now. Yes, he's my brother, but how about calling me when they're down there so I can decide if I want to see them or not. That's what I pay for." He hung up.

I pulled away from the door as small footsteps moved toward it. The door opened, and I saw the smallest human I'd ever seen. Wherthman would have stood a head taller if they were side by side. I noticed that, like Wherthman, he was well proportioned. He didn't look deformed in any way, but he sounded it.

He let out a stream of "fucks" and "assholes" and

some colorful additional things about sex and bowel movement. It was a small education.

Peese wore a fancy white embroidered shirt and a soft sweater. I would have spent more time looking at him, but I noticed something else as we stepped into a large room. All of the furniture was scaled down to his size. A door was opened in the wall and I could see into the bedroom. It, too, was scaled down.

He turned and sat in a small dark armchair. His face was childlike, but there was ancient anger on it. He was one of the small, bitter people of the world. Some of them are six feet tall, but their palms sweat; they keep their heads low and turn them only briefly upward as they pass you with the sneer of the cornered animal unsure of whether to bite or cry. He lit a cigar and said, "Sit down."

I wasn't sure where to sit. The couch was too small and the little table in the room too fragile looking. He watched my awkward search for a perch and smiled viciously. He puffed at the full size cigar and leaned back.

"You don't get many full size visitors?" I asked, deciding to sit on the floor. The carpet was dark green and soft enough.

"I get them all sizes," he said.

"I get it," I went on, placing my hat on the floor and my back against the wall. "You like full-sized people to feel awkward and clumsy in here."

"You're a smart man, Penis," he said with a grin.

"The name's Peters, John Franklin. Remember it and I'll remember not to step on you," I said, returning the grin. Wherthman had told me that my brother Phil had used that line on him. It had done wonders to ruin

Wherthman's disposition. I wished the same on Peese, but I didn't get it.

"Well," he said puffing away, "I feel awkward most of the time in your houses, your buildings. I enjoy having people like you feel foolish."

He had a point, but I wasn't going to start giving him points.

"I do keep a few bloated chairs for friends," he said. Since he didn't run to a closet to fetch a chair, I assumed I wasn't in the elite company of his friends. But, after all, we had just met.

"It's been pleasant getting acquainted with you, John Franklin, and I hate to cut off this stimulating conversation, but I have a few questions."

"I don't have any answers," he puffed. The room was getting smokey and smelled like leftover cow's breath. I wanted to get out as fast as I could.

"Let's try," I said, shifting my weight on the floor. "Why did you kill Cash?"

A cloud of smoke cleared, and I could see his eyes. I wondered if I could defend myself against a knife attack from him while seated on the floor. No knife came out.

"I didn't kill him," said Peese. "Didn't know he was dead. Sorry to hear it."

"You sound like you'll never recover from the shock."

"I'll get over it," he answered.

We made a fair act, but I wasn't sure which of us was Bergen and which was Charlie McCarthy.

"What business were you in with Cash?" I tried.

"We weren't. I knew him."

"What business are you in?" I pushed on. He didn't

answer. I wanted to go flat on my back, but that would have made me too vulnerable. "This is a pretty nice place. You live in a fancy hotel, bring in your own furniture, smoke big cigars, wear fancy clothes. A few months ago you were cadging nickels to make the rent in a Main Street flop. Moving up in the world, ain't you, Rico?"

His face turned red, but it wasn't going to be that easy to get him. He was still talking, which meant maybe that he knew something. He might be my man or one of them.

"I do some acting," he said, leaning back and blowing a cloud in my direction.

"Pays real nice, doesn't it? What've you been acting in? *Oz* finished shooting over a year ago, and that didn't make you rich."

He squirmed a little, but not much.

"I don't have to give you a list of credits," he said. "You got better questions?"

"You got better answers? What about the fights you had with Cash?" I stood up. I'd lost the battle to try to appear comfortable. He could have that one.

"Who says we fought?" Peese shouted. "We were pals. We didn't fight."

"You don't seem all broken up over the death of your pal," I said, hovering over him. He looked up, but he didn't look scared, just mad.

"Who said I fought with Cash?" he insisted.

"Wherthman. Gunther Wherthman," I said.

He laughed and pointed his cigar at me.

"What would you expect him to say? He's trying to put the murder rap on someone else and picked me. He didn't like Cash, and he doesn't like me."

It was my turn to smile.

"Why would Wherthman want to put the rap on you?" I asked innocently, just oozing with curiosity.

"Because the cops know he did it," said Peese through his teeth.

"Where'd you hear that?"

"You told me when you were out in the fucking hall."

I said no, and he tried again.

"I must have heard it on the radio or read it in the papers."

I said no again.

"That's all I've got to say," Peese said, standing. "Now get out and don't come back, and if you tell the cops anything about what I said, I'll swear you made it up."

I started toward the door and tried one more trick.

"Someone else saw you arguing with Cash," I said. "Saw you Friday morning at Metro just before Cash was killed. Identified you."

"Who?" he demanded, grabbing my sleeve. I looked down with my best serious face.

"A guy named Grundy, a photographer," I said. "Identified you right down to your angelic voice."

Peese exploded and stamped on the floor. He reminded me of a childhood picture of Rumpelstilskin. I thought he was going to put his foot into the ceiling of Apartment 809.

"That double-crossing bastard!" he shouted. "That muscle freak is lying."

"Be seeing you," I said, opening the door. He rushed at me and threw a punch at my groin as I turned to wave to him. The punch hit me in the stomach, and I tumbled back into the hall on my back. He slammed the door. There wasn't much I could do about it. I'd come up with some information, but I'd paid for it by being laid out by a midget.

My wind came back slowly after three or four good gasps. Then I went to the door to listen. I could hear Peese asking the telephone operator for a number. I couldn't make out the number he asked for. We both waited for what must have been a dozen rings. Peese hung up with a bang, and I pulled my ear from the door and limped to the elevator.

By the time I dropped to the sixth floor and a lady with purple hair got on with a purple dog in her arms, I knew a few things. Grundy was probably the guy who had taken the shots at me. He was the only one of the three witnesses who had heard the two midgets arguing on Friday morning. He had identified one of them as having an accent and being called Gunther. Gable's testimony about the size of the two midgets might put a small hole in that. How many German accented midgets named Gunther could there be in L.A.? But I wasn't sure it was enough. If Grundy and Peese were in on something together, as soon as Peese talked to Grundy, he'd be calmed down again. With his temper, though, I doubted if Peese could go through an hour with my brother without giving everything away.

All I had to do was dump the information in my brother's lap and hope he'd pull in Grundy and Peese and put them in different rooms. I had no idea of which one of them had actually killed Cash or why, but I didn't much care, either. Phil could worry about that.

When we got to the lobby, the purple dog snapped

at me, and the purple lady gave me a dirty look. The desk clerk picked up the look, and I picked up Chandler, who was calmly leaning against a wall watching the people walk in and picking up the atmosphere.

"Get any good dialogue?" I asked.

"Fair," he said, putting his pipe away. "What about you?"

As we headed out to the street and under the hotel canopy, I told Chandler that Peese looked like the man I wanted, and that a muscle-heavy photographer seemed to be in it with him.

"And you're going to turn it over to the police?" he asked. "You're not going to try to find out why Cash was murdered, or why they tried to kill you and Judy Garland?"

"They tried to kill me because I was putting the pieces together to prove Wherthman didn't do it," I explained. "They figured my next step was to Peese, and they were right. My curiosity ends there."

It wasn't exactly the truth, and something still gnawed at me. Chandler's detectives were probably full of germs of curiosity and covered with the poison ivy of responsibility. Those diseases could get you killed in my business. It was still a mess, and I wasn't sure Phil would or could pull it off with what I had; but short of trying to force a confession out of Grundy, I was finished. If a forty-five-pound midget could flatten me with a single punch, what would Grundy do to me? He might not be able to shoot straight, but there was nothing wrong with his hands.

I was facing out toward the street when I saw the woman. There were a lot of people walking in both directions, but she had stopped and was looking up. She had a big brown paper bag in her arms and a look on her face I'd never seen. Her hand went to her mouth and the package fell. She had just been to a Chinese carry-out place. The little white cartons exploded on the sidewalk. Shrapnels of rice and egg roll flecked the unwary. I stepped out from under the canopy and looked up. Someone seemed to be hanging out of a window in the hotel. Someone else was not helping him get back in. It was hard to look up into the sun, but the lady and I saw that much. Other people were looking up now, too.

About fifty people saw the hanging man fall. He tumbled over in five or six circles without a sound before he hit the top of a passing Sunshine Cab and bounced off onto the sidewalk about fifteen feet from me. The body almost hit the purple lady with the purple poodle. I don't know what Chandler did, but I stepped forward a foot or two to be sure the body was Peese's. It was, though he'd be hard to identify by anything but his size and the clothes he was wearing. His face had hit the Sunshine Cab on the way down.

I turned to Chandler, who looked grim but controlled, as if he had always expected to see something like this, and life had proved him right.

"That's Peese," I said, and ran back into the hotel.

People were pushing past me to get out and see what had happened. Someone asked me. I pushed and ran for the door marked STAIRWAY. I pulled out my .38 and started to run up the stairs two or three at a time, listening for footsteps above me. The killer might take the elevator, or he might take the stairs. I didn't know how many stairways there were in the hotel. I doubted if he would risk attracting attention by going down the fire escape. I also gambled that he wouldn't want to cut off his options by using the elevator.

Somewhere I guessed wrong. No one came down the stairs. By the ninth floor I was winded, but my handball hours and running kept me up, and my back didn't scream. No one was in the hall. It would take a few minutes for someone to figure out what floor Peese had flown from. The desk clerk would identify him, and the cops would be coming. Peese's door was open. I stepped in, not expecting to find anything or anyone; I was right. The window was open and I had no intention of looking out. I put my gun away and looked around the place quickly, not worrying about prints. I had visited the place earlier and there were witnesses to it. There was also a witness to my being on the sidewalk when Peese went flying. Chandler's testimony would probably be good enough even for my brother, but I didn't wait to be tied up explaining things. I hurried through the place and found a closet. It was open, and a little chair stood inside. I stood on the chair and looked where someone had apparently looked a few minutes before. Standing on the chair, I was eye level with a shelf. I turned on the closet light. The shelf was empty but the dust showed the outline of a circle the size of a big plate.

I got down trying to figure what might be shaped like that. I kept figuring as I left the apartment and headed for the elevator. When it opened, the desk clerk I had talked to in the lobby was on it. So was a uniformed cop complete with cap, dark tie, long sleeves, and a serious look on his freckled young face. They stepped off, and I stepped on.

The doors were closing when I heard the clerk say, "That's him. The man who was with Mr. Peese."

The young cop turned to me too late. The elevator doors closed. He had a few choices. He could run down the stairs and stand a good chance of heading me off if the elevator made any stops. He could call the lobby and have someone try to stop me. If he were really stupid, he'd wait for another elevator. I counted on him taking about fifteen seconds to make up his mind unless he was really a sharp rookie. He didn't look all that sharp. I put my luck on the elevator instead of getting out and running down.

My luck held. No one got on the elevator, and I hit the lobby in about fifteen seconds. The lobby was almost empty, except for a few people looking out of the windows at the body. Everyone else was already outside. Chandler spotted me hurrying through the door and stepped over to me.

"I think I saw your man," he said. He described Grundy right down to the biceps and bleached hair.

"Was he carrying anything?" I asked.

"Yes," said Chandler. "A can, a big tin can. Looked something like a giant nickel."

"About two feet across?" I asked, looking back over my shoulder for the cop.

"Yes," he said. "What was it?"

"Film," I said. "Movies. Whoever killed Peese took the film from the apartment."

Chandler scratched his head and pushed his glasses back to keep them from falling.

"What's on the film?" he asked.

"I don't know," I said, "but I know who to ask."

I took his hand, shook it, and thanked him for his help. I also told him that I might be needing his help with the police. The crowd around Peese's body had reached riot size.

"Of course," he said. "You're going after the killer?"

I shrugged, and he looked pleased. I was doing what private detectives are supposed to do. I was walking the mean streets. I was acting like a damn fool.

7

GRUNDY HAD A can of movie film and, for all he knew, all the time left in his life to put it away. He didn't know I was behind him. With luck I might even get to his place before him, if that's where he was going.

He wasn't going there. I parked on Highland and went to his door. It was open. The upstairs door wasn't. I knocked and prepared to greet him with a gun in my hand, but he didn't answer. I listened at the door and heard nothing. I could have jimmied the door without much trouble, but what I was looking for wasn't there. I wanted Grundy and that film. He was probably driving around with it in his trunk. I didn't even know what his car looked like though I'd seen it twice, once when he took a shot at me on Normandie and once when he was pulling out of the Happy Byways Motor Court after trying for me again.

I went back to the restaurant where I'd watched him eat. The frizzy waitress was there, and her face was blank. She probably hypnotized herself into not thinking or feeling till the work day was over. The trouble with that was eventually the hypnotism doesn't wear off at quitting time, and you're like that all the time. It happens to waitresses, senators, movie stars, and cops.

I ordered a coffee from her while I sat at the counter and remembered too late that the coffee there was awful. It was late in the afternoon so I added a tuna sandwich and a grilled cheese on white. Nothing much was going on in the restaurant. It was well past lunch and too early for dinner. An old guy with thick glasses and a cigarette stuck to his lower lip sat at a back booth reading the newspaper and nursing a coffee and roll. He was the only customer. The frizzy waitress had her elbows on the counter next to the cash register. She looked at the window, but I didn't think she saw anything.

"I was in here the other day with Barney Grundy," I reminded her.

She got off her elbows and looked at me, trying to place me. I've got an easy face to remember, but she couldn't place it. All she had seen was Grundy, but he wasn't here now.

"You a friend of his?" Her head tilted to the side like a curious bird. A touch of rouge that hadn't been absorbed stood out on her cheek. She looked like an unfinished clown, and I felt sorry for her.

"We've been spending a lot of time together," I said, finishing the grilled cheese first because it was hot. "He's really something."

"He sure is," she said, a smile touching her face.

"Come in here a lot?"

"Just about every day," she said.

"I was just over at his place. He wasn't there." I

started on my tuna sandwich. It had too much mayonaise, which is just how I like it.

"He's working out down at Santa Monica," she said. "This is the time every day. I thought you were his friend. You're a friend, and you don't know that?"

"I'm a business friend," I said. "I work for M.G.M. and I've got to reach him about a film he has. If I can find him fast, it could mean a big difference in his life. You know the name of the place in Santa Monica where he works out?"

She looked at me suspiciously, and I went on drinking my coffee without looking at her. I looked at my watch.

"I've got to be back at the studio with an answer tonight," I sighed. "I'd sure like Barney to get this chance."

"Cimaglia's," she said. "Cimaglia's Gym on Main."

I said thanks, forced myself to finish my coffee slowly, overtipped, and went out onto La Brea. There was a drug store on the corner. I went in and headed for the phone booth.

The first call was to Andy Markopulis at M.G.M. I described Grundy and told him Grundy was probably our man. He said he'd get the word to Woodman and Fearaven, who were still keeping an eye on Judy Garland.

Then I called my brother.

"Toby," he said too calmly, "I've been looking for you. I'd like you to come over to my office for a little talk."

"I'll be over as soon as I make a stop," I said just as calmly. "I know who killed Cash. He also killed another midget named Peese about an hour ago."

"That's what I wanted to talk to you about, Toby," Phil's voice said slowly. "We've got a desk clerk who gave us a pretty good description of you. Seems you were in Peese's room when he took the fall. A cop saw you, too. Now I remember you saying you were looking for a midget. I'd like to have the officer take a look at you. You mind coming down here?"

"I wasn't in the room when he was tossed out," I said. "I was on the sidewalk watching a woman spill her Chinese dinner. I've got a witness."

"Fine," said Phil, the familiar edge coming back. "You just come in here, and we'll talk it over."

"The killer is Grundy. Barney Grundy. Your witness who saw Wherthman talking to Cash on Friday. Grundy, Cash, and Peese were in something together, something to do with movies."

"This town is running out of midgets," said Phil. "It'll be a lot safer for little people if you come in here. Now I'm getting tired of asking you."

His voice was up to its familiar level of rage, and I was glad he didn't know where I was.

"I'll be right there," I said.

"You've got thirty minutes," he said, and hung up.

I looked up an address in the phone book, found my Buick, pulled into traffic, almost hitting a new Chrysler, and headed in the opposite direction of my brother's office. Santa Monica wasn't far, and I wanted to talk to Barney Grundy.

Cimaglia's was a one-story white brick building a block or so from the beach on Main. This Main Street was not related to the Main Street where Peese had flopped until his sudden wealth. Los Angeles is a jigsaw puzzle of over 140 towns jammed next to each other.

There are over 800 duplications of street names. After forty-four years I still got lost once in a while. Cimaglia's didn't look like a gym from the outside, but inside it looked like a training center on Krypton. Behind the small counter stood a guy about five-six. He was about fifty and built like a smaller version of Grundy. He wore a blue tee shirt over his muscles, and his black hair was cut short like a field of grass. He had a towel over his shoulder and identified himself as Cimaglia. Beyond Cimaglia was a big open room with about ten guys built like Grundy. Some were pumping chucks of iron on pulleys; others were lifting weights. There wasn't much sound other than some panting and the clank of metal. Whatever they were doing, they were serious about it.

"What can I do for you?" said Cimaglia. I didn't see Grundy among the grunters in the room.

"I'm looking for Barney Grundy," I said. "I'm a friend of his, and he has something for me."

"Left about five minutes ago," said Cimaglia. "Didn't stay long. Just did the weights."

"Did he say where he was going?" I asked.

Cimaglia said no.

"Did he have anything with him?" I tried.

"Just his bag," said Cimaglia, who saw something in the room beyond that he didn't like, so he shouted, "Slower Rocco, slower! A lot slower."

Cimaglia watched Rocco for about a minute, and when he was satisfied he turned to me.

"Wait," he said. "Barney had something else with him. A big round tin box."

"He brought it in here?"

"Yeah," he said. "I think he left it in his locker."

The locker room door was behind Cimaglia, and my

mind moved fast. I had figured Grundy for a cool killer who had calmly thrown a man out of a window and then went to his favorite gym for a workout. It didn't fit with the nervous killer who kept botching attempts on my life. Grundy had come to Cimaglia's to hide the film he had taken. For some reason, possibly the fear that the cops or I might search the place, he hadn't taken it back to his studio home. He probably didn't trust anyone to hold it for him. A locker at Cimaglia's would be a perfect place to put it.

The problem was getting into that locker.

"Thanks," I said, turning for the door.

"Want to leave a message in case Barney comes back?"

"Yeah," I said. "Tell him Peese is looking for him."

"Will do," he said, turning to watch Rocco.

There was a window in the outer door of Cimaglia's, and from the street I could see the counter and Cimaglia looking back into the gym. I hung around for ten minutes, keeping an eye on Cimaglia and trying not to look too suspicious to the guy in the gas station who stared from across the street.

One of the muscle builders came out, and I said hello to him. He said hello back and headed down the street. I looked back through the window, and I could see Cimaglia moving into the gym. I went back in, holding the door so it wouldn't make noise, and watched Cimaglia move to a far corner to show a sweating Hercules how to curl a bar of steel.

I moved along the wall near the door and ducked into the locker room. It was smaller than I expected. Just enough room for two benches and two rows of lockers. There was a toilet in the corner and a stall with two showers. The locker room was clean and empty with a few spots of water on the floor where someone had dripped after showering.

The lockers had pieces of adhesive tape on them and a name in ink on each piece of tape. Grundy's locker was in the corner near the shower. I moved fast, not wanting to be caught in there, but I knew I had to deal with the lock. I put the barrel of my .38 into the loop of the lock and tugged. Nothing much happened, but the top of the locker did give a little. I pulled again with one hand and got a few fingers into the space at the top of the locker. I pulled some more and wormed a few more fingers in. The locker snapped against my hand but I kept the space open. I put the .38 away so I could have two hands working. In about twenty seconds I had worked up a sweat, but I had a good two-handed grip on the top of the locker.

The locker bent a little when I pulled. Luckily for me the lockers weren't built for high security, just for privacy. I did my best to violate that privacy and finally did with a grunting tug that snapped the latch. The lock didn't break, but the door banged open. It made a lot of noise. The can I was looking for sat on top of a pair of shorts behind an orange towel that had been drapped over it. I tucked the can under my left arm and stood up.

There was one door to the locker room. I had come in through it, and now Cimaglia stood in it. Behind him stood Rocco and there was another bulky body behind him.

"What're you doing?" asked Cimaglia.

I was fresh out of lies. I pulled out my .38 and pointed it at him. He didn't seem to notice.

"Grundy stole this film," I said. "Now I'm stealing it from him. If you want to take a bullet for someone else's can of film, that's your choice."

"That's not much of a gun," said Rocco. The sweat was still on his forehead and darkening his tee shirt. He was right. In that space and with his bulk it wasn't much of a gun.

"If you shoot it right," I said softly, "it can make a nice little hole in someone's face. And I can shoot it right. Now just back away from the door, and I'll leave. You can tell Grundy what happened, but I don't think he'll call the cops."

They didn't back away. Charlie and Rocco took a step forward. I wasn't about to shoot two citizens trying to keep me from stealing something, but I had a sudden vision of what that small army of muscle could do to me. I leveled the gun and shot. The bullet crackled next to Cimaglia's ear and slammed into the plaster wall behind him. Cimaglia stopped moving.

"I meant to miss," I said, "but I'm running out of bullets and getting nervous."

"I can see that," he said. A slight grin touched his face, and I think he liked the way I was handling the situation. "O.K.," he said with a lift of his hand. "Back up and let him out."

They backed up reluctantly and I moved through the door. I could see that Rocco didn't like to back up for anyone.

"If you're lucky, you'll never meet any of us again," Cimaglia said.

"I'll try to be lucky," I answered, backing out of the front door. My car was a few feet away, and I got into it, dropping the can on the seat next to me. Cimaglia stepped out of his door, but he was in no hurry. He just watched me pull away. I waved to him, but he just stood there with his hands on his hips, shaking his head.

After a mile or so, I pulled over and put the film in the trunk. It was getting late, and I had some choices to make. I could get to my brother fast and tell him I had car trouble. Or I could just turn the film over to him and let him find out what was on it. I could go back to Grundy's place and talk to him. I could do a lot of things, but I headed for M.G.M.

I wanted to see what was on the film.

The faces at the gate were unfamiliar, but I gave my name and they called Cassie James, who was on the lot. She vouched for me, and I drove in and over to Judy Garland's dressing room, where Cassie met me, wearing solid green. She touched my arm and gave me a soft kiss.

"I've got some film to look at," I said. "Where can we set it up?"

While she arranged for a projectionist and a projection room, I told her about Peese and Grundy and the film. She asked me what it all meant. I told her I didn't know, but maybe the film would tell us. Cassie went to tell Judy where she'd be, and I tried to hold up the film to the light, but I couldn't tell anything.

She came back, held my arm, and stayed close while we walked around a few buildings and into a small one with a projection booth and a couple of armchairs.

An old projectionist Cassie called Lyle threaded the film in the booth and sat back. We turned off the lights and looked at the screen. Blank white film shot through, and Lyle focused on some numbers. There was no sound. The first image was a scene from *The Wizard of Oz*, with Judy Garland in a yellow wig.

"They shot a few weeks of Judy in the yellow hair," Cassie explained, "but they decided it looked too phony."

The next shot was of two male Munchkins holding hands and walking into a house. The Munchkins were dressed as a soldier and a lollipop kid. The film was in color, but the quality of the color was nothing like the first shot. The two Munchkins went into a house and saw a girl lying on her stomach in bed. The girl was wearing the Dorothy costume and had long yellow hair.

The Munchkins leered at each other and began to take their clothes off. The girl on the bed turned and covered her face with her hands. She didn't look anything like Garland, but the hands across the face hid enough of her to make it clear that the girl in the first shot and this one were supposed to be the same.

The Munchkins leapt on the bed and began to undress the girl.

They hadn't gotten very far when Cassie James said, "Stop."

I flipped on the lights and shouted to Lyle to turn off the film. Lyle was obviously not watching. I stepped in front of the screen, and the image went over my body. A naked Munchkin was on my chest. Cassie looked at me frantically, and I shouted again. This time Lyle heard and turned off the projector. He came out of the booth as I took Cassie's hand.

"What's wrong?" he said.

"Nothing," I said. "We've seen enough. Just wind it back and give it to me."

Cassie shuddered next to me. "It's horrible."

And that, I thought, was only the beginning. We had seen no more than a few minutes of what looked like fifteen minutes or more of film.

"It explains a couple of things," I said. "Grundy, Cash, and Peese were in business together making pornographic movies. They stole film, used sets when they could. Cash must have wanted more money, and they killed him, trying to blame Wherthman. I was getting too close so Grundy tried to kill me. When I got onto Peese, Grundy knew he might accidentally spill something, so he threw him out the window and grabbed this film. Grundy told me he wanted to be a cameraman. This is how he was doing it."

Cassie said nothing, just held my hand. Then she spoke.

"But why did he call Judy to find the first body? And why did he try to poison her?"

I didn't have an answer, but it was a good question; and I'd put it to Grundy when I found him.

Lyle gave me the film and I thanked him. It was almost dark and Cassie led me to her office, which was really more like a workroom full of costumes, measures, scissors, and drawings. There was a couch in the corner. The room wasn't really very big and it was among a series of similar rooms, but the rest of the building seemed empty. She turned out the lights and came close to me, leading me to the couch.

We sat in the dark on the couch for a long time saying nothing. Then we made love. I forgot Grundy and my brother for a while, but the while was too short.

"I've got things that have to be done," I said.

"I know," she said.

"You want me to take you home first?"

"No," she said, taking my hand. "I've got my car. Call me when something happens, and take care of yourself."

I walked her down to her car, which was parked on the side of the building, and I headed back to my own, parked near Judy Garland's dressing room. It was dark. There were lights in a few offices and the sound of activity on a stage not far away. I passed two women in fluffy costumes talking about someone named Norman.

I opened the trunk of my car and dropped the film in. When I closed the trunk I heard something behind me.

"Just open it again," said Grundy.

I faced him. He was wearing a thin jacket and a .45 automatic. He stepped toward me. I opened the trunk and pulled out the can.

"Meant to ask you something the next time I saw you Barney. Is Nimble really your middle name?"

He didn't answer, just reached out for the can after shifting the gun from his right to his left hand. The gun was in the wrong hand and he was a rotten shot. If I didn't do something, I was sure I'd be joining Cash and Peese. His hand was almost touching the can when I brought it down as hard as I could on the gun. The .45 flew into the dark, and the can rolled after it. Grundy was nimble. He was on me before I could get the .38 out. I bounced back into the trunk and kicked up at his face. He stumbled backward. As I came up I lost my .38 in the trunk. I groped for it, but Grundy pulled me out and my back cracked against the ground.

He stood over me, breathing heavy. Blood was trickling out of his nose, and he didn't look too pleased with me.

"Let's talk," I gasped.

He shook his head no and picked me up as if I were a Shirley Temple doll. He was going to kill me with his hands and fists, and he was going to enjoy it. I punched him low in the stomach, but nothing happened. I threw a knee at his groin, but he twisted and took it with his calf. His right hand tightened around my throat, and he pushed me back hard against a nearby wall. My head screamed in pain, and I went out.

There was a tunnel in front of me, and I jumped into its darkness, followed by grinning flying monkeys. My old pal Koko the Clown took my hand and led me tumbling into the darkness to a little black and white shack. A cartoon version of Grundy, bouncing muscles, lifted the top of the shack, exposing me and Koko. Behind Grundy was a skyful of flying monkeys. Koko took my hand again, and we raced across a frozen lake with Grundy and the monkeys in pursuit.

Koko and I jumped into a bottle of ink and pulled the top over us. We swam in cool darkness, safe and protected.

8

T HE MOON WAS swaying gently in the sky. It was a
dull red against the darkness. I watched it, almost
hypnotized. Something was behind the moon, but
I ignored it. I had never seen the moon swaying before.
The thing behind the moon became clearer. It was a
face. Not only did I have a murderer to deal with, I had
to figure out why the moon was swaying and why there
was a face behind it.

A streak of pain hit my head and I moaned. I was
lying on my back and the floor was cold under me. I
pushed myself up in pain and touched my head where
Grundy had banged it against the wall. My hand came
away wet and sticky.

The moon was red because my own blood was dripping into my dazed eyes. I looked at the moon again
and the face behind it became clear; it was Clark Gable.
Then more of the moon mystery was solved. The moon
was a small light bulb dangling from the ceiling, rock-
ing gently in front of a portrait of Clark Gable. The bulb
didn't give much light, but I could see a sky full of
paintings in front of it and behind it.

The pain and blood told me I probably wasn't dead. By straining with the information I was getting, I figured out that I was on the floor of a big prop room.

When I tried to stand, I went back on my knees and leaned against something that was not quite a prop. It felt like a human knee. My hands found the rest of the body, and I could tell from what I felt that it was Grundy or someone else who had spent a lot of time worrying about his body. Whoever it was had no more earthly worries. A knife was sticking firmly in his chest.

With a lot of effort and some help from a table, I pulled myself up and held the light bulb toward the body. It was Grundy. His eyes were opened and startled. As far as I could see, there was no trail of blood on the floor. It looked as if he had been killed where he sat.

In contrast, there was plenty of blood where I had been lying on the floor. It was my blood. My mind was working well enough to tell me to get the hell out of there, but my head wouldn't cooperate. There seemed to be a kind of aisle going past Grundy's body. I made my way along it, feeling past furniture and props as I went.

In a few thousand years, I reached the door of a freight elevator, which I managed to get open. I got myself inside and leaned against a wall, not knowing if I was up or down. I pushed all three buttons on the wall and the elevator moved. When it stopped, I staggered out. It was almost dawn, and I wanted to get somewhere where I could think. If Grundy was the killer, who killed Grundy?

Whoever did it had saved my life, but I had little else to thank them for. They'd left me with a corpse. I couldn't figure out where I was on the lot, so I wandered around for about ten minutes. Then I saw Hoff's office and made it to my car. Someone was leaning on it. Someone else was standing next to the leaner. The guy leaning on my car was my brother the cop. The guy with him was Sergeant Steve Seidman.

I stopped, waiting for Phil to rush at me and lay me out with a right to whatever part of my body least expected it. He did move toward me quickly, but there was no punch. I must have looked great.

"What the hell happened to you?" he hissed between his teeth.

"I got fresh with Joan Crawford," I said, and fell forward in his arms.

I didn't quite go all the way out this time. Events took place over and around me in a kind of soup as the sun rose. Officer Rashkow appeared from nowhere, and Phil told him to get an ambulance. Seidman was told to try to figure out where I had come from. Phil picked me up and brought me somewhere, but I couldn't make it out. Then Judy Garland's face appeared above me.

"Mr. Peters? Oh, Mr. Peters, are you all right? Will he be all right?" She sounded scared and concerned and I wanted to reassure her, but I couldn't talk.

Then I felt myself lifted and traveling. There were sirens, and I wished they would shut up so I could rest.

When I opened my eyes again, the sun was bright above me, but it wasn't the sun, it was the ceiling light in an emergency room. The face above me was familiar. It belonged to a kid named Dr. Parry who had fished that bullet out of me not long ago. He was dressed in white and had blonde hair and glasses. He was sewing my scalp.

"You are a stupid man, Peters," he said, sewing away. "Your head is a battleground of contusions and fractures. The human body is not built to take this abuse. That head's going to come open like an egg one of these times."

"How bad is it?" I asked.

Neither he nor I could make out what I said. I tried again slowly. "How bad?"

"Concussion, hairline fracture, fifteen stitches," he said. "Maybe sixteen."

A nurse stood next to him and said nothing. She reminded me of my father's favorite reading lamp—tall, thin, and white.

When he'd finished, they helped me up. My jacket was gone, and my shirt was bloody.

"You'll live again," said Parry, cleaning his hands in a sink. "You think you can tolerate our company long enough to spend a day here while we watch you for any little problems like brain damage?"

He didn't wait for an answer. I was placed in a wheelchair, and the nurse built like a lamp wheeled me into the hall. Phil was standing there with his arms folded and displeasure on his face. I closed my eyes in agony.

A guy with a Southern accent x-rayed my head none-too-gently while chewing gum. The nurse wheeled me back down the hall past Phil. Doc Parry checked me out and asked me to do some tough things like following his finger with my eyes and telling him my name and address. I passed the test.

"You are a mass of scar tissue shaped like a man," he said, "but you're probably all right." He nodded and the frail nurse wheeled me back in the hall. Phil followed us down a corridor and into an elevator. No one spoke. We went up to a room and the nurse helped me into a gown. Her touch did nothing for me, and I apparently did nothing for her.

"You want these kept?" she said, holding my bloody clothes up for me to see.

I said no and laid back on the bed. As soon as my stitched head hit the pillow I shot up in pain. Phil was leaning against the window.

"We found Grundy," he said. I turned on my stomach and groaned. "You're doing great, Toby. We've got you for two murders, Peese and Grundy. Your prints are on the knife, aren't they?"

"You tell me," I said.

"I'm telling you. You've done some stupid things in your life, but yesterday may mark your all-time high. I told you to come to my office, and you went after Grundy. What happened? He push you around, and you stabbed him in self-defense?"

"No," I said. "I went out when he cracked my head. When I woke up, he was sitting in front of me with a knife in him, just like Cash, the one on the Yellow Brick Road. That suggest anything to you, like the same murderer?"

"I thought you said Grundy threw Peese out the window?"

"Right," I said. "It had something to do with pornographic movies Grundy was making with midgets. He was stealing footage from M.G.M. and . . . Did you find that roll of film?"

"Toby, Toby," he said moving toward me, "there was no roll of film. The main witness we had against the little Nazi . . ."

"He's Swiss . . ."

". . . is dead," continued Phil. "The best alternate suspect, Peese, is dead. You were with both of them before they died. You argued with both of them. You are up to your ass in trouble."

"Search Grundy's place," I said. "Maybe you'll find some names, numbers."

"Anything worth getting, you've got," said Phil. "You went over that place fast and messy."

"You mean someone went through Grundy's things?"

"You know it, Toby."

Phil put his hand on my leg and started to squeeze. The nurse came in.

"I'd like some rest now," I said.

"I'll see you a little later, Toby," Phil said, pushing past the nurse.

"That's my brother," I told her. She didn't look impressed.

In the hall I could hear Phil asking the nurse when she came out how long I'd be laid up. She said I wouldn't be able to move for a day at least.

There was a phone next to the bed. I called Shelly Minck, told him to get to my place, get my last suit, put it in a bag, and come to the hospital. I also told him to pick up a clean white smock, and come up to my room. If anyone asked him, I said, he should identify himself as Dr. Minck.

"That's who I am," he said.

"Then you won't be lying," I answered and hung up.

The nurse came in with a pill and a newspaper for me. I pretended to take the pill, and I took the paper. It told me that 50,000,000 people were expected to vote today. It told me that the first election results were from Sharon, New Hampshire, where Willkie had taken the lead 24-7. On the next page, a Japanese Ambassador named Yoshiaki Muira from Japan said the United States and his country would not fight over China.

It took Shelly over two hours to get to the hospital. He hadn't changed into a clean smock, and he came in waving his cigar. The important thing was that he came in and he had a small black suitcase with him.

The room bounced me around while I dressed, and Shelly kept talking about root canals. I almost threw up, but managed to keep it down.

"See if you can get a wheelchair," I said.

I sat on the edge of the bed waiting for the nausea to pass while Shelly was gone. He came back with a chair, and I climbed in. He pushed me into the hall and down the corridor, talking all the time about tooth decay. I hoped no one stopped to listen to him. We made it out of the hospital with no problems, and Shelly helped me to his car. I didn't know where mine was. My gun was either in the trunk or Phil had it, unless the killer had gone through the trouble of getting my keys when I was out, then getting the gun and putting the keys back. I doubted it, but what the hell did I know.

Shelly drove around, squinting through his glasses, while I tried to think. His driving was a series of near misses which he didn't seem to notice. It was hard to think.

Somewhere about 8000 on Sunset he pulled to the curb. His Ford was a '37 in only slightly better shape than my Buick. I took one of the pain pills Shelly gave me and watched while he bought a map to the stars' homes. The seller was a guy sitting under a big umbrella. He rocked back and forth on a wicker rocker and had his feet up on a chair whose back had been sawed off. He was in no hurry. He might not be making much money, but no one was trying to kill him. I thought about asking him for a job. I'd take the chair without a back.

Shelly drove on looking for Jack Benny's house. Somewhere beneath the stitches my brain was working. An idea was coming.

Shelly turned on the radio, and we found out that Hank Greenberg, the Detroit outfielder, had been named Most Valuable Player in the American League. Twenty minutes later we stopped at Awful Fresh MacFarlane for a twenty-nine cent pound of candy in a paper bag. We were somewhere between Union and Hoover, and I asked Shelly to look up an address for me. He found three listings for a James Cash. I borrowed some change from him and went into a bar. What I really wanted to do was go home, but too many people knew where that was. I couldn't even go back to the office.

The Cash idea was a longshot, but I didn't have any short ones. My head felt better with Shelly's pill inside me, and with a hat on I looked almost respectable. I called the first James Cash. It was a Venice number. James Cash answered, and I said he was the wrong one. I called the second in Burbank, and a woman with a very small voice answered. I asked for James Cash, and she told me he was dead. I asked if he was the same James Cash who had worked in *The Wizard of Oz*, and she said he was; she agreed to see me.

Shelly was tired, and I was feeling better, so I dropped him a block from the office. He wanted to work for a few hours more. We agreed that I'd return his Ford later. He reminded me to vote, and I told him I'd try.

"Go with a winner for a change, Toby," he said. "Willkie."

I made it out to Burbank on one more pain pill, a Pepsi, and two chicken tacos. It was a little after noon when I pulled into a driveway next to a sign that read VISIT OUR FURNISHED MODEL HOME. The Ford bumped through the field toward a quartet of small, white wooden homes. They were lined up in a field of mud. Each one was exactly like the one next to it. Some of these developments could line up the little homes for miles. This one was just getting started.

The house I was looking for was on the end. The view must have been terrific from the inside: nothing but rubble, telephone poles, and dirt that had broken the monotony last night by turning to mud.

Cash's little woman was a very little woman. I leaned over to shake her hand. She was kind of chunky with a pleasant face and dark hair, probably in her thirties. She led me into a living room with normal size furniture and went out to get me a cup of coffee and a piece of banana cake.

"How can I help you?" she said.

"I'm working for M.G.M.," I explained. "We want to find out just what happened to Mr. Cash."

"I told the police everything I knew," she said, "but it didn't seem to help."

"Everything?" I said. The cup shook slightly in her little hand. There was no toughness in her, and I wanted to go easy.

"You want to tell me about the movies he was working on?" I said softly.

She started to cry, and I let her. The banana cake was good. I had a second piece and indicated that I would appreciate another cup of coffee. She was happy to get it for me. When she came back, she sat on a chair in front of me. I could see from the brand that she wore children's shoes.

"James didn't know I knew about what he was doing," she said, "but I knew. I think he was trying to get out of it, and whoever did it didn't want him to."

"You think he was going to the police?" I said.

"He didn't exactly say so, but Thursday night he said we could move back East soon." The tears were coming back. "James had a difficult life. We were only married a few months ago. We wanted children, but all we could afford was this. He was ashamed of what he was doing, Mr. Peters."

If he was ashamed of it, he was damned good at hiding it if the porno pictures I saw were any evidence, but the lady deserved her grief.

"I'm sure he was, Mrs. Cash," I said, patting her shoulder. "And you didn't tell the police any of this?"

"No, I didn't think it would do James' memory any good."

"You did the right thing," I said. "Did the police look through your husband's things?"

She said they had, but she had held out one thing from them, an address book he kept hidden.

"I knew those addresses were of the people he was working with."

"One of them might have murdered him," I said.

"They probably did," she said, "but finding the killer won't bring James back, and letting everyone know what he was involved in might get back East."

"And you're going back East?"

"Yes," she said. "My parents live in Missouri. They're

not little people. They're getting old, and they want me back. I haven't got anything but this house, and it's not paid for. If James was getting a lot of money for what he was doing, he had it put somewhere I don't know about."

She got me the notebook and asked me to promise not to tell anyone where I got it. In return for the book I promised to try to keep Cash's name away from any pornography publicity.

She shook my hand, and I went outside. The sky was dark in the North. Maybe a twister would come and lift Cash's house out of the mud and carry it over the rainbow. Maybe elephants would shit diamonds.

Glendale was a few minutes away so I drove to my ancestral homeland and went into The Elite Diner, a block away from the police station where I had once worked. The counter man knew me, and we said hello. He had once been a cop, too. He showed me a stomach scar he had picked up since I last saw him, and I showed him my head. He said I was the winner and brought me some coffee; I didn't want anything with it. Most of the names in Cash's little green notebook didn't show anything I didn't already know. Grundy's name was in it. So was Peese's. There were others I didn't recognize, probably old friends. Maybe people in the business with him. There were a couple of numbers after initials. One of them struck me as familiar. I looked at it for a while until it blurred and came back into focus.

Night was coming over the mountains. I thanked the ex-cop and drove slowly toward the setting sun. Everything fit now. It didn't make sense, but it fit. All the tinkertoy facts built into a tower of truth, an ugly tower built by a sick child, but it was hard to turn away from.

The drive back took about an hour. I should have been in a hurry, but I wasn't. No matter how the day ended the next one would look dirty. Maybe Raymond Chandler had been right about the shoddy merchandise and shoddy people. Maybe old Toby Peters and his optimism were finally dead. Maybe Toby Peters would stop laughing at the crap he lived in. Maybe.

9

I MUST HAVE caught the election day shift at Metro. I didn't recognize either of the guys at the gate. I asked if Warren Hoff was still there and told them to give him a call. Hoff told them to let me in, and I headed for his office. More and more of my time was being spent at M.G.M. at night. Pretty soon I'd be able to find my way by feel.

Hoff's secretary was gone for the day, but Warren was well-trimmed and seated in his desk chair.

"Well?" he said.

"Not very," I answered. I sat in the chair across from him and put my hat on his desk.

"I heard about what happened last night," he said. "We're going to have a hell of a time keeping two murders quiet. Mr. Mayer will just have to understand."

"Keeping the murders quiet is the easy part, Warren my friend," I said. "The hard part is catching the murderer."

"The police think you did it," Hoff said. He got up and poured himself a drink. This time he offered me one, but I said no.

"No, they don't, Warren. They just find me handy to have around for unsolved crimes and a place for their bloodhounds to piss if the hydrants aren't available. They don't think I did it."

"Who do they think did it?" His voice was calm.

I don't know," I said. "They're running out of suspects. Every time a good one crops up he gets himself killed. But I think we can end all that."

I threw the green notebook to him.

"What's this?"

"A new list of starlets from central casting. Check the number on page fifteen, near the bottom."

He flipped through the book and found the page. He recognized the initials and the number. The notebook came flying back to me, and I speared it before it went for a hit into center field.

"Whose book is that?" he demanded.

"James Cash."

"The dead midget?"

I told him he was right, and he said he didn't believe it, that there had to be some explanation. There was one, and he and I knew it.

"You want to help me find a roll of film?" I said, heaving myself out of the chair. He didn't, but I knew he'd come along. I led the way, but we both knew where we were going.

We turned on the light when we got there and began to search. He wasn't trying too hard, but I was enjoying the mess I was making. There was a shelf of old books, a low shelf I hadn't seen before. One of the books, a huge, oversized one, looked funny. It was old-new with a brown, wood-like color and yellowing crisp pages. The book must have been two lifetimes old or more, but some of the first pages hadn't been cut. The centers of the middle pages were cut out, and a roll of film nested neatly inside. The film was no longer in a can or on a reel. It was on a core to keep the weight down. I closed the book and handed it to Hoff.

"Well?" I said.

"Not very," he answered.

My opinion of Hoff had changed four or five times in the few days I had known him. I thought he was taking it all pretty well now, all things considered.

We walked outside. The night air felt colder than it had when we went in. Hoff held the book against his chest to prove it was there and for warmth.

"You want to tell me about it?" I said.

"No," said Hoff, "but I will. I just can't believe what this implies."

"It doesn't imply anything," I said. "It proves it. Maybe not good enough for a judge and jury, but good enough for anyone who can add with two hands. Cassie James killed Grundy and Cash. There's no other answer. Now, what can you contribute to the cause?"

Back in his office, he poured another drink and told his tale. Cassie had gotten close to him, very close to him. Close enough over the period of a year to get him to help her smuggle out pieces of film and to get him to let her use certain sets for a film she was doing. As a publicity executive, he could explain that it was all part of a publicity campaign. Besides, she never wanted to use anything that was in demand.

Hoff didn't know exactly why she was doing it. He was told that it was part of a scheme to get cheap screen test reels for young actors. The actors would be able to take finished reels around with them when they applied for jobs.

"It sounded innocent enough," he said. Hoff was on his third drink when he said it, and the words were starting to run together.

"It was a lousy story," I said. "She didn't even bother to make up a decent lie."

"I know," said Hoff, "but I believed her. I wanted to believe her, and she didn't make a big thing out of it. It was all kind of casual."

"You must have thought something was up when Cash was found dead."

He admitted that he had and had wanted to talk to Cassie about it. That was why he had been so nervous on Friday morning when he met me. While I was talking to Judy Garland, Cassie was outside the door convincing him that she had nothing to do with the death of the midget.

"She made me feel like a fool for even asking," he said. "Why would her screen test idea lead to murder? It was just two midgets who were to be in a screen test with a young actor. The midgets had fought, and one of them had killed the other one. She said if I told about the screen test business we'd both lose our jobs and for nothing. The film had nothing to do with the murder. She can be very convincing, Peters."

I knew how convincing Cassie James could be. She had convinced me into corners for three days. I fed her everything I knew, and she had Grundy try to take me out. She even had him get Peese when I got too close. Hoff was an amateur idiot compared to me.

"Where is she now?" I asked. Hoff didn't know, but he said he'd try to find out. I thought he was too drunk to handle the phone, but he became a changed man with the phone in his hand. It was his tool and, drunk or sober, he knew how to handle it. He started calling places on the lot where she might still be, but he came up blank. Finally, someone on the set of *Ziegfield Girl* remembered that Judy Garland had said she was going to dinner with Cassie James.

"O.K., Warren. Here's what I want you to do," I said, popping a pain pill. I hoped they weren't addictive. "You call Cassie's house. If she's there, try to find out if Judy's with her. Got that?"

"What else?" he said soberly.

"That's all. Cassie put the poison in that water pitcher to harrass Judy. Cassie had Grundy or Peese call Judy Garland on Friday and tell her to go to the Munchkin City set. Cassie James does not like Judy Garland. You got that straight?"

He got it straight. He didn't have to look up the number in the green notebook or his own. I only got his side of the conversation, but he was worth listening to.

"Cassie," he said happily, "how are you . . . Yes . . . No, I'm just clearing up a few things here . . . Yes . . . the police are sure that Grundy killed both midgets and Peters killed Grundy . . . I am, too . . . Cassie, I was wondering if I might come over tonight. It's been a while . . . oh, sure. I understand. No, not at all. Give her my best." He hung up and turned to me. "She's there."

I got Andy Markopulis on the phone. He was at home. The guys who were watching Judy Garland had no radio in their car. Even if they were outside of Cassie's place in Santa Monica, they'd never think she was in any danger inside. They'd work at keeping people out.

"Warren," I said. "Go home. I'll call you as soon as I know anything."

The drive to Santa Monica took about fifteen minutes. I ran lights and kicked well past the speed limit. When I got to Cassie's house, the lights were on. I cut my lights and let the car glide in neutral down the hill. The sound of the surf covered the clinks of the Ford. I wanted a surprise knock or a chance to sneak in and get Judy Garland out. If Cassie saw me coming, she might use her knife act again.

Everything was going well. I parked against the shadow of a hill and got out. Moving as slowly as I could, I went down to the beach and into the sand to approach the house from the ocean. I was about ten feet from the porch leading to the beach when they jumped me. They were both good at that. One hit me high. The other low.

The surf covered the sounds of our grunts and groans as we rolled over, getting sand in our ears and eyes. My main fear was that my stitches would open. I wanted to end the fight before that happened.

I got to my feet by backing away on my behind and starting to run. Then I turned on them. Their faces were clear in the moonlight. One of the two wore a smile and was rangy. The other one was solid. The rangy one got to me first. I put both of my hands together in a double fist and drove them into his stomach. He went down with an "ooph" sound. The second guy hit me running, and we tumbled over again. I threw my elbow into his neck and he groaned.

I stood over them, gasping for air.

"You two Woodman and Fearaven?"

The rangy one got to his knees and said he was

Fearaven. The only fight I'd won in weeks had been with two guys on my side. I helped them both up, telling who I was, giving Andy's name and showing my wallet. It convinced them, but they were all for rushing the house and taking Cassie by surprise. I admitted that it might work, but convinced them there was a better way.

The better way involved my walking up to the front door and spinning a tale while they found a way in through the back. If Cassie wasn't armed, there was no problem. If she was, we needed the surprise.

We brushed each other off and moved. I went up the beach to the front of the house. I couldn't see Wood-man and Fearaven, but through the window I could see Cassie and Judy Garland seated at the table near the window. They were having coffee, but the dishes weren't cleared yet and there was a steak knife in front of Cassie.

Cassie's color for the day was brown. Judy Garland was wearing a skirt and fluffy blouse. Her hair was in pigtails, probably to contrast with that grownup role she was living in her movie and probably trying to live in her life.

I knocked three quick raps and stood back to see the reaction. It wasn't what I wanted. Cassie didn't get up. She just shouted, "Come in!"

The door was open, and I stepped in.

Cassie smiled at me with a look of true love. Judy Garland looked slightly surprised.

"Sorry to drop in without calling," I said, "but I need help." I plopped in a chair.

"Can I get you anything?" said Cassie, with a voice filled with concern.

"I could use a drink," I said.

Something in the way I said it must have tipped her off or made her suspicious. Her voice had changed, dropped a tone or two when she said, "It's by the wall. Help yourself."

Judy Garland had fallen for the act and started to get up, but Cassie firmly motioned her to sit down. The motion was maternal and friendly, but to deny it was to disobey.

"What are you doing here, Toby?" Cassie demanded. "The police are looking for you for the murder of that man Grundy."

Judy Garland rose a little in concern.

"Mr. Peters, did you?"

"No," I said, "but I know who did. So does Cassie. Don't you, love?"

"I have no idea," she said, looking as perplexed as innocence should look. I almost faltered. Maybe I was all screwed up, seeing things that weren't there, backing away from a show of commitment.

"You killed Grundy, Cassie."

Cassie laughed, and Judy Garland's mouth dropped open. Cassie poured herself a fresh cup of coffee from the steaming pot in front of her and asked if I wanted some. I said no.

"Cassie, what's he talking about?" Judy said, looking at both of us and wondering why we were so calm in the face of flying accusations. Judy had never played this one before.

"Let's tell stories," I said. "You want to start, Cassie?"

"I think not," she said, sipping her coffee and throwing back her head. The gesture was perfect. The light caught the black of her hair and sent out moonbeams.

"O.K., I'll start. You, Grundy, Cash, and Peese were in business together—the porno movie business. Everything was going well until one of your partners wanted to know why his share of the profits was so low. I've seen the way Cash lived. If there was gravy in this, he wasn't getting any. He found out that Peese was living high, and they argued on Friday morning just before Grundy was set to shoot a scene. Cash started to talk about getting out, about telling the cops or M.G.M. You couldn't have that so you put a knife in him. Right so far?"

Cassie didn't answer. She just looked at me tolerantly. Judy's eyes were wide and fixed on her.

"You and Grundy worked out the scheme to frame Wherthman," I went on. "Peese must have remembered that the two of them had picked on the Swiss bookworm. The foul-up came when Judy called me, and Mayer thought I had connections. When I got too close to figuring out that the calls to Judy and to me were by someone without an accent, and couldn't be Wherthman, Grundy panicked. I can't see you breaking under so little pressure, but Grundy would. Then I started to get close to Peese. It was pretty clever of you to come up with his name and give it to me. You knew I'd get it from Wherthman or someone around the studio. You got more information out of me the other night, too. I think you were really surprised the first time I told you that someone had tried to kill me."

"I was surprised," she said softly.

"But the second time, when Grundy followed me to Hearst's Castle, was no surprise. I told you where I was going. You gave him the information. He botched it again. Then I got to Peese a little faster than you expected. Grundy was right behind me. What was Peese holding over you to rate that place downtown—the film?"

Cassie just kept drinking coffee.

"Well, Grundy got the film, and I was in the wrong place at the right time. You started to figure that it was only a matter of time till the cops or I figured out that Grundy was involved. When I got the film from Grundy, you made up your mind. You got me to the studio, called Grundy, watched a few feet of the porno film with me and pulled your shocked act. I think the act came so I'd stop looking at the picture. I have a feeling there's something on that film that connects you to Grundy, Cash, and Peese."

"Like what?" she asked innocently.

"Like maybe this house being used as a location?"

She stiffened enough for me to see, but she didn't break. I didn't think she would.

"I'll go on. You had Grundy waiting for me at my car after you lulled me to sleep with your soft couch and body. Grundy was ready to kill me, or I'd kill him. You would have been all right either way. When he knocked me out you didn't know whether I was dead or alive. You had Grundy carry me to the prop room, and then you repeated your knife act. You got rid of Grundy, and if I didn't die, chances were good that the cops would blame me. You had the roll of film and there were no witnesses. But, Cassie, the cops were bound to start turning up people you used in your movies. And how long did you really think you could fool Hoff?"

That got her. She put the cup down. I got up as if I were stretching my legs and kept talking.

"Now all this would be good guess work on my part if it weren't for one thing."

"And what's that?" asked Cassie.

"I talked to Hoff and we found the film, exactly where you hid it."

She thought I might be bluffing, and she said so.

"A big brown book in your office," I said.

"I see," she said.

"Can I ask you one question or two, Cassie?"

"Yes," she said sweetly.

"Why did you want Judy to find the body? Why did you try to poison her? And what the hell did you get into all this for? You don't need the money."

Cassie looked at Judy calmly, and I took a few steps toward them as if I just wanted to hear what was being said.

"I hate her," said Cassie with a thin smile.

Judy started to rise, and Cassie picked up the knife. It was sharp, long, and in the hands of an expert.

"Sit down, Judy," I said calmly. She sat down and kept her eyes fixed on me. Cassie's eyes were fixed on the girl in front of her as she spoke.

"She got what I deserved, what I worked for. I had the looks and the talent. I still do, but I didn't have the luck. I got over it, though. I had a second chance through my sister. My kid sister was even better than I was, and I put everything I had into her career. I bought costumes, publicity. I set up parties, gave her lessons. She was doing fine. In another year she would have made it. We both would have made it, but she lost a part to Judy. It wasn't much. She," Cassie said, nodding at Judy, "probably doesn't even remember it or my sister's name: Jean James."

I could see by Judy's face that the name meant nothing to her.

"She lost another part to you, too," Cassie went on, her lips getting thinner and her brow tighter. "Then she began the drinking and the pills. I warned her, but in less than a year her looks were almost gone. She tried to live a lifetime in one year. She died two years ago in a car crash. I have no more sisters."

"I've got another explanation," I said. "Got it from a doctor named Roloff. Your jealousy of Judy has nothing to do with your sister. You're jealous of her success because you see it as sexual success. So you take men who come near her, and you turn out porno movies that ridicule her. I'll bet you even appear in the movies."

"You're dirt," she hissed at me as I took a step toward her. She moved quickly to Judy's side and put the knife at the girl's throat.

"You don't need the money," I said. "You need the excitement; the sex and the sexual substitute. You needed the next substitute, murder. You started putting that long knife into men. Was I next, or was it Hoff? I don't think you even know, do you, Cassie?"

"I'll have the satisfaction of killing her," Cassie said, her eyes glaring at me.

I could see Woodman and Fearaven out of the corner of my eye. Woodman had a gun in his hand, but I knew he couldn't take a chance. He'd have to be good to be sure he wouldn't hit Judy. There was nothing much we could do but wait while I tried to keep her off balance.

At least that's what we thought. While I was trying to dig a new track out of my head, Judy suddenly threw the coffee pot at Cassie James. I hadn't seen it, but the girl had been reaching her hand out for it while she did her fear act. Cassie screamed and looked ready to plunge the knife. I leaped forward and fell a few feet short on the table. Woodman took a shot and missed. Time was frozen. I waited for the enraged Cassie, coffee dripping from her hair and eyes, to move forward. But it was Judy Garland who moved. She threw her elbow into Cassie's stomach and pushed the woman away from her. It was an act of rejection I would have liked to make, but wasn't sure I could have.

The knife hit the floor, and Woodman and Fearaven were on Cassie. She turned, suddenly calm as they lifted her. She was a wet, dripping mess. Her beauty was still there, but it was ruined by her makeup, which looked as if it had melted under strong lights.

"I trusted you," Judy said quietly.

"I hated you," Cassie said, without looking at the girl.

I called my brother while the two men held Cassie. Then I took Judy out and into my car.

"It's like a bad dream," she said.

I agreed. It was like a bad dream for both of us. I wasn't sure whose loss was greater, but since I'd lived longer I gave her the benefit of the doubt and hoped her life wouldn't be a series of disappointments from people she put her trust in.

On the way to her house, she told me she was thinking of getting married. She said he was a composer or bandleader named Rose. I'd never heard of him, but I told her I hoped he was a good man. When I drove up in front of her house, she leaned over and kissed me.

"I'm glad I called you, Mr. Peters." Then she ran out of the car and up the walk.

I wasn't so sure I was glad she called me. I'd lived a lifetime in three days. At least Cassie's sister had a year. My pay for the trouble would be some bad memories and about $300 from M.G.M. My body told me to pull over and go to sleep, but my mind reminded me of what happened the last time I'd slept in a car. My brother would find me if I went home, and Shelly was probably at the office wondering what the hell happened to his car. I could go to a few people to be put up, but a better idea came to me.

In fifteen minutes I was back at the hospital. A woman at the front desk tried to stop me. She said visiting hours were over. I told her I wasn't a visitor; I was an in-patient.

The elevator took me up slowly, and the lampshade nurse met me when the doors opened. Her face was lined with professional anger and a look of betrayal.

"Where were you?" she asked.

"Saving Judy Garland's life," I said, and walked into my room. I flopped on the bed in the dark and fell asleep.

There were no dreams of flying monkeys, muscled maniacs, or Koko the clown. There was only darkness, which suited me just fine.

10

WHEN MY EYES opened on Wednesday morning, Franklin Roosevelt was sure of another four years in the White House, but I didn't know that for a while. What I knew was that someone had taken my clothes off and put a gown on me, that a termite in my head was trying to get out the hard way, and that my brother and Charlie Cimaglia, the little muscle man, were looking down on me.

I moaned pitifully and tried to turn over, but Phil wasn't about to let me.

"Let's talk, Toby," he said.

"Can't," I said, letting out a fearful groan.

"I'll punch you in the back so hard your kidney will turn to mud," he whispered.

I turned back over and sat up on my elbows.

"Let's talk," I said.

"This the man, Mr. Cimaglia?" he said.

The man with all the muscles looked at me without anger and said I was the man.

"What was in the can, Toby?" asked Phil.

"Movies," I said. "Mostly stuff stolen from Metro. I returned it to them."

"The charge wasn't theft," said Phil. "It's assault with a deadly weapon. You took a shot at Mr. Cimaglia and threatened his life."

"I don't remember threatening his life, and I was five feet from him when I shot. If I wanted to hit him, I would have hit him. Hell, I did him a favor. I got Grundy out of his place. He should be giving me a reward."

For some reason, this amused Cimaglia, who laughed and said, "You got balls, Mister. You really have."

"You want to talk to a lawyer, Toby?"

"My lawyer's name is Leib, Martin Leib . . ." I began, but I didn't finish.

"Hold it," said Cimaglia putting up his hand. "I made a mistake. This isn't the man." Cimaglia looked at me with a grin.

Phil turned toward Cimaglia, his hands in tight fists, his belly rumbling. There wasn't much room in there, but I sat up to watch the battle if it came. I'd say it was even. Cimaglia was much smaller and a little older, but he had muscle. Phil had anger and a lot of experience hitting people. The battle didn't come. Phil unclenched his fists and told Cimaglia to get out. He did.

"Cassie James confessed to the murders of Cash and Grundy," Phil said, resting his big rear against the window ledge and folding his arms. "With you, Woodman, Fearaven, and Garland, we didn't need her confession, but it helps. Now, there's no trial."

"And," I continued, "no need for publicity? No need to mention M.G.M., Gable, Garland?"

"No need," said Phil. "That woman doesn't like you, Toby."

"Yesterday I thought she loved me."

"Look in a mirror," he said. "She says you tossed Peese out of the window."

"You believe her?" I laughed. "Not even you would believe her."

He pushed away from the window and pointed a finger at me. "Not so chummy, Toby. It doesn't matter what I believe, does it? We've got a case against you. Now, who is this writer who can give you an alibi?"

"Chandler," I said. "His name is Raymond Chandler, and he lives someplace in Santa Monica. He's listed."

"Same Chandler who wrote *The Big Sleep*?" asked Phil.

"You heard of it?"

"I read it," he said. "A lot of bullshit. Read it. You'll love it."

He stopped talking and circled the room a few times. I watched. There was nothing else to do with the back of my head as sore as it was, unless I turned my back on him, and I wasn't going to do that with my brother. Something might upset him and give him the idea of a parting chop at my kidneys. He stopped pacing and turned to me.

"Toby, you're a little old, but I could swing it. I can get you on the L.A. force. Detective, at the bottom."

It was one of my dreams. I was sure of it, but he didn't move. I turned my head a little. The pain was still with me. I was awake.

I'd been a cop before, and I didn't like it. I didn't like worrying about what the guy above me thought about what I was doing. I didn't like having to be somewhere every day and tell someone where I was all the time. I didn't like someone else deciding on whose misery I had to live with. The pay was steady. The power felt good, but you had to give up too much. I knew I wouldn't take it.

"I'll think about it Phil. Thanks," I said.

He knew I was saying no, and the hurt showed in his eyes as rage. He didn't know how to show any other emotion to me, and he didn't like having opened himself even a little. It must have taken a final push from Ruth, my sister-in-law, to get him to actually come out with it.

"I'll really think about it, Phil," I said.

"You'll wind up a bum, he said. "You're close to it now. What happens when your legs go and you don't think so fast anymore?"

"Then I'll be qualified to become a cop," I said. I knew I shouldn't have said it, but I couldn't resist the opening. Phil came at me around the bed, but he didn't make it. The door opened as Jeremy Butler and Shelly Minck came in. Even Phil thought twice about assaulting a patient in his bed in front of two witnesses.

Phil turned his back on me and pushed past my two visitors.

"My brother," I said.

Butler nodded knowingly, and Shelly paid no attention. Under his jacket Shelly wore his once-white smock. His cigar was out, and I asked him to please leave it that way.

"Shelly," I said, looking as ill as I could, "I'm sorry I didn't return your car yesterday, but things got out of hand." I gestured to the room in explanation, but Shelly had seen the room before, and he wasn't impressed.

"Slept in the office," he said. "It's all right. I brought your car. The cops told me I could pick it up and bring it to you, Here's the key." I took the key and told him to get his out of my pants' pocket.

"Thanks for coming to see me, Jeremy," I said.

He shifted uncomfortably. The shift was massive. Something was troubling him, but I didn't want to push him.

"Mr. Peters." He always called me "Mr. Peters." "I have some sad news for you. Your bungalow is being demolished today. The city condemned the property. All the houses in the court will be flattened."

"Can they do that to you?" I asked.

He said they could, but they also had to pay for it, and they were paying a lot more than the property would be worth for at least twenty years. They were talking about putting up a fire station on the site. Butler didn't care.

"All your stuff is in your car," Shelly said. "Someone broke your windows. So I jammed it all in the trunk."

Somehow that sobered me for a second. I remembered that everything I owned could fit in the trunk of a '34 Buick.

"We'll help you find another place," Butler said. "I've got a friend with a place a few blocks from downtown, not far from the office."

"I'll look at it," I said. "Thanks."

Butler probably didn't know I was turning him down. He hadn't been dealing with me for over forty years the way Phil had. Some time in the few seconds since Butler had told me my place was being flattened,

I had decided to gain a little respectability, find a reasonably decent apartment, maybe acquire a little property. My mind didn't tell me how I was going to do this with my income, but it made me feel noble to believe I was going to try.

Doc Parry came in while Shelly was telling us that Mr. Strange's single tooth was a marvel and that he was considering bridgework to go around it. Strange would have a mouthful of teeth anchored to Shelly's monument. The whole job would be worth a few hundred bucks, which Shelly would have to put up himself. It wasn't kindness towards the bristled bum that prompted Shelly. It was pride. He'd make up the few hundred by shoddy work on other patients.

Parry listened to him for a few minutes with a sour face of disgust. He shook hands with Butler and turned his back on Shelly, who didn't seem to notice. Butler and Shelly left after telling me where my car was, and I said I'd give them a call.

Parry ran his left hand through his thin blonde hair. He was in his twenties and would be bald in five years. He took my pulse, listened to my heart, examined my head, told me I was a fool—which I already knew—and said I could go home. I didn't have a home, but I didn't tell him that.

"Remember what I said about that head," he said at the door. "It can't take too much more of this."

I got dressed slowly, picked up my hospital bill, and went to my car. My face bristled with beard, and my mouth was dry. I opened the trunk of the car. It wasn't even jammed. Under the cardboard suitcases I found my .38. No one had even noticed it.

Before going to the office, I stopped for something to eat at a drive-in that offered three jumbo fried shrimp for a quarter. I drank a Pepsi, ate a taco, looked at the sun, and listened to the people in the next car talk about the election. They knew all the time that Roosevelt would win again.

Breakfast over, I went back to the office. Butler waved and dragged a bum toward the alley. The hall still smelled of Lysol, and our waiting room still hadn't been cleaned. Shelly had a patient waiting, an incredibly skinny young woman carrying a baby. She didn't look like big money. The patient in Shelly's chair didn't look like big money, either. It was another bum.

"Phone call for you," said Shelly over his shoulder, shifting his cigar.

The call was from Warren Hoff.

"Warren," I said when I reached him. "It's all over." He said he knew.

"Thanks for keeping me out of it," he said. "I destroyed the print, but there may be other prints around."

"There may be," I said. "I'll bring you a bill for my services later." I was tempted to give him more advice about going back to a newspaper, but who was I to give advice? I'd just turned down equally good advice from my brother. Maybe Warren Hoff was smarter than I was, but I doubted it. Our experience with Cassie James was evidence.

"Could you come in this afternoon, Toby?" he said. "Mr. Mayer would like to see you."

I said I would and that I'd drop off my bill with him.

In the next hour I shaved and worked on the bill and came up with this:

Fee: $50 per day for five days	
(minus $50 advance)	$200
New windows for 1934 Buick	40*
Payment for information	10
Hospital room and expenses	37
Replacement of ruined suit	25*
Telephone	3.50
Motor court, one night	7
Holy Name Church of God's Friends	1
Food	11
Parking	.50
Gas	8
Total	$343.00

*Estimated expenses

I had a feeling I had missed something, but I wanted the whole thing over with. I clipped on the hospital bill, a parking stub, and a receipt from the Happy Byways Motor Court, and put the bundle in an envelope. The only envelope I could find had Shelly's name on it, complete with the D.D.S. and the S.D. The S.D. didn't mean anything. It was something he had made up to look impressive. At least the return address was right, and it was the only one I had.

I was getting up to leave when Gunther Wherthman came through the door. His mustache was gone, and he wore a smile.

We shook hands, and he found a way to get on my chair with dignity. He politely did not look at the office, nor comment on it.

"I should like to thank you for what you have done, Mr. Peters," he said. His suit was neatly pressed, and the bruise from my brother was fading.

"That's all right," I said.

"I should like to pay you for your services. For your time and trouble. What is your normal fee?"

"M.G.M. is paying me, Mr. Wherthman," I explained.

"Nonetheless," he said, reaching for his wallet, "I wish no charity from M.G.M."

Even I could recognize dignity when I saw it, though I hadn't seen much of it around Los Angeles. I knew Wherthman was just getting by and anything he gave me would cut into his rent or lunch, but I wasn't going to deprive him of what he wanted.

"Ten bucks," I said.

"That is very little for what you have done," he said, counting ten singles out, "but I must admit if it were much more I should have to owe it to you." He got down from the chair, and we shook hands.

"Can I buy you dinner tonight, Mr. Wherthman?" I asked. He said he would be delighted, and I said I'd pick him up at his place around seven.

"I've got to make a stop at M.G.M. and then look around for a place to live," I explained. "I just lost my last place."

"There is, I believe, an opening in the house in which I am living," he said. "If you would be interested. It is clean, quiet, and on a nice street. The landlady is pleasant, and the rent is reasonable."

I thanked him for the idea and said I'd think about it. There was nothing to read into my answer this time. I really meant to think about it. It might not be exactly what I had thought about a few hours earlier, but it was a step in the right direction, and I liked Wherthman's company. His dignity might rub off on me.

My stitches were tight when I stepped into Shelly's office. He was working on the skinny lady. Mr. Strange of one-tooth fame was holding the woman's baby and making faces at it. It was his God-given talent. The baby loved it.

The drive to M.G.M. was pleasant. I only thought of Cassie James and what she had done once or twice. The rest of the time I thought about my next meal, the money from Metro, and my future.

Buck McCarthy was on the gate, and we jawed for a few seconds until a car pulled in behind me. Greer Garson was in it, her red hair blowing in the slight wind. She pulled next to me, and Buck waved her in. She smiled at me, and I smiled back. Everyone was smiling today.

"Adios," I said to Buck, and he smiled.

Hoff's secretary gave me a pleasant South of the Border smile and told me to go in. Hoff pumped my hand and thanked me. I accepted a ginger ale with ice, and he looked at the bill.

"Looks reasonable," he said. He went into his pocket and pulled out four 100-dollar bills. They were crisp and new and I took them.

"We'll just even it out," he said. "I'll get reimbursed when I turn in your bill."

We wanted to say something else to each other, but there was nothing to say. What we shared we didn't want to talk about, and there was a hell of a lot we didn't share. So I drank my ginger ale, and he drank something dark with ice in it. I said I had to go. He reminded me that Mayer wanted to see me. I hadn't forgotten.

We walked back to Mayer's office, and he left me. He said he hoped we'd see each other again, and I said the same, but neither of us meant it.

This time I had to wait for Mr. Mayer. Someone was with him. I tried to talk to Blonde No. 1, but she acted busy, as if she had misplaced her desk.

I spent half an hour looking at the photographs of the studio's stars on the walls. Then the door opened, and Mickey Rooney came out with a tall, dark man wearing a dark suit and carrying a briefcase. Rooney was grinning and rubbing his hands. He almost danced out. The shoulders on his suit were too wide. I expected him to say, "Oh, boy, oh, boy" in glee, just like Andy Hardy.

He recognized me and said hello, but he couldn't put a name to my face. A lot of people can't. I told him who I was and reminded him that I had worked a premiere or two as security.

"You working here full time now?" he asked.

"No," I said. "Just temporary."

"Too bad," he said, grinning. "It's a classy dump."

The tall man with him said nothing. Rooney bounced away smiling. It was a classy dump.

The blonde led me through the door and turned me over to the redhead; then to the second blonde, who led me into Mayer's office. He was talking to a woman in a grey suit about redecorating the office. I thought it was a good idea, but I didn't say so. I sat in the same comfortable white chair without being asked and waited.

"I want it to stand out and yet be subtle," he told the woman, who nodded to indicate she understood.

When she left, Mayer came around the table, and I stood up. He pumped my hand a few times and looked into my eyes.

"Words can hardly express how much I appreciate what you've done, Mr. Peters," he said.

"Words and cash," I said. "I've been paid, and I've been thanked."

"Do you know who was just in here?" said Mayer. "Mickey Rooney. He's a good lad, a little excitable, but a good boy. This studio has a reputation for good, wholesome entertainment, and you've helped to keep our image clean."

He was overdoing it, but that was his style when he wanted something. I'd learned that from my last trip into the huge chamber. I had nothing left to give him, and I couldn't imagine Louis B. Mayer holding me up for a kickback from 400 bucks.

"So," he said, "how would you like to become part of our organization?"

It was my second job offer of the day, but I turned it down. I'd worked security for Warner Brothers for enough years to know I wouldn't want to go back to it. It had the same drawbacks as being a cop, with none of the advantages except slightly higher pay.

Mayer hadn't really expected me to accept, and that wasn't what he had on his mind. I think part of his social interaction was to offer jobs to people he liked.

"It's been nice talking to you again, Mr. Mayer," I said getting up, and he looked surprised. I guess people didn't walk out on him very often; they waited till he was finished.

"You're a pusher, aren't you?" he said, standing behind his desk. I shrugged. "I've got a job for you," he said. "A job for you in your own line."

"Fifty a day and expenses if I take it," I said quickly. He brushed that away with his hand, and indicated that I should sit down. I sat and he leaned over his desk.

"How much do you know," he whispered, "about the Marx Brothers?"

"Well, in a few minutes I shall be all melted, and you will have the castle to yourself. I have been wicked in my day, but I never thought a little girl like you would ever be able to melt me and end my wicked deeds. Look out, here I go!"

With these words the Witch fell down in a brown, melted, shapeless mass and began to spread over the clean boards of the kitchen floor. Seeing that she had really melted away to nothing, Dorothy drew another bucket of water and threw it over the mess. She then swept it all out of the door. After picking out the silver shoe, which was all that was left of the old woman, she cleaned and dried it with a cloth, and put it on her foot again. Then, being at last free to do as she chose, she ran out to the courtyard to tell the Lion that the Wicked Witch of the West had come to an end, and that they were no longer prisoners in a strange land.

L. Frank Baum
The Wizard of Oz

AFTERWORD

by
STUART M. KAMINSKY

TOBY PETERS WAS born a creature of two loves. I love movies. I love detective stories.

"Father, I want to confess," says Kansas, the dying cowboy in Dennis Hopper's *The Last Movie*.

"What is it, my son?"

"The movies," whispers Kansas.

I know how he feels. The movies.

The first movie I remember seeing in a theater was *Gunga Din*. I couldn't have been more than five years old. I loved the Movie Theater, the long torn-down Crawford on Chicago's West Side. It was a palace of exquisite kitsch, with its carpets and twelve-foot-high, gaudily colored statues of Nubians. Compared to the one-bedroom apartment my parents and I, along with my aunt and cousin, lived in, it was better than caramel-coated popcorn. And the movie itself, *Gunga Din*, drew me in with a combination I would forever love—adventure, terror, and comedy. Sitting next to my mother and father, my love of the movies was immediate and obsessive.

From that night on, I begged my parents to take me to the movies. I learned the names of stars. Within a few years I began to learn the names of minor character actors, writers, directors, art directors, and cinematographers. I became a walking miniature encyclopedia of the movies. I never lost that love, that ability to leap into a movie and rest comfortably in the tale, surrounded by tinny sound, the smell of buttered popcorn, and the scratches at the start of each reel. And then to come out of the dream and worship the men and women who had created it for me.

Eventually, that love led me to earn a Ph.D. in film studies, with a minor in theater from Northwestern University, so I could earn a living talking about, writing about, and teaching about what obsessed me—the movies.

The second movie I remember seeing was *The Cat and the Canary*; not the original silent version, but the one with Bob Hope. I thought I was going to see *The Wizard of Oz*. My Aunt Bess had dropped me off alone at the Metro Theater on Lawrence Avenue. I was six. As soon as the credits came shivering on, I ran from the theater, screaming for my aunt and shouting "The Cat and the Canary!" I found her halfway down the block. She guided me back and assured me that Bob Hope was funny and the movie was a comedy. I think she had shopping to do. I went back in. Terrified, I watched. I loved it, almost as much as I had loved *Gunga Din*.

The following week, I did get to see *The Wizard of Oz*. Again, I was dropped off. I always sat in the tenth or twelfth row, I would have liked the first row, but that was where the troublemakers sat, making bad jokes, throwing popcorn and jujubes, looking for smaller kids like me to bully.

In the darkness on that afternoon, I fell in love with Judy Garland. I have, since that afternoon, seen Dorothy, Toto, the Wizard, the Tin Man, the Scarecrow, the Cowardly Lion, and both witches dozens of times. Now, when my family and I watch the tape of the movie, I am under oath not to say the lines with the characters.

I can't resist.

"Are you a good witch or a bad witch?" I ask along with Billie Burke.

"Dad."

I don't know how many people I've asked that question. From the age of six I gradually learned to resist the impulse to divide the world into either good witches or bad witches. It is a much easier world to deal with if there are only good or bad witches.

I shut up. I go into another room to read or watch a baseball game. I start thinking. I confess. I almost weep. I want them to live again: Dorothy, the Scarecrow, the Tin Man, and my favorite, the Cowardly Lion. Were you in the room with me now, I'd gladly subject you to my rendition of "If I Were the King of the Forest," complete with Bert Lahr tremolo.

When I wrote the book you have before you, I lived in Chicago. Now I live in Sarasota, Florida, where I discovered a wondrous thing: Sarasota is the original home of the Ringling Brothers Circus. Many of the actors who played Munchkins retired here. Not many are left, but there are a few. I see one in particular from time to time. She's a regal little woman who played one of the members of the Lullaby League. She has a little poodle who reminds me of Toto.

When I wrote this book, I wanted to bring them all back, all the characters I had first seen when I was six. I wanted to make it all happen again in the movie of my imagination. What I came up with, as I always do, was a collision or a collusion of genres. Dorothy meets a private eye. Still aided by her three protectors, she manages to defeat the Wicked Witch.

Movies are not better than life. They *are* life. The essential part of life that feeds the hungry imagination.

My best friends when I first learned to love the movies were Cary Grant, Lloyd Nolan, Warner Baxter, Clark Gable, Gary Cooper, Charles Starrett (The Durango Kid), Wild Bill Elliott, William Powell, and my stuffed monkey, who I creatively called Monkey. Monkey became every villain I had seen on screen—the flying monkeys, Victor Jory, Charles Middleton, Yakima Cannut, Kurt Katch, Douglas Dumbrille. I mercilessly pummeled Monkey till he lost his tail.

Even as an eight-year-old my favorite movies were shown as part of a triple bill on Saturday afternoons. The A-movies were of little interest. I liked Westerns and Laurel and Hardy, but I loved detective movies— Lloyd Nolan or Hugh Beaumont as Mike Shane, Chester Morris as Boston Blackie, George Sanders as the Saint, Tom Conway as The Lone Wolf, Warner Baxter as The Crime Doctor, Basil Rathbone as Sherlock Holmes, and either Warner Oland or Sidney Toler as Charlie Chan.

It more than pleases me that my eleven-year-old daughter's favorite movie character is Nick Charles, and that she knows all the *Thin Man* movies almost word for word.

Ah, now back to my second love, detective fiction.

My father read only detective stories, pulps, and magazines. He had piles of them. After one of his twelve-hour days at the luggage factory or in the mom and pop grocery he half owned with my uncle, my father would soak in the bathtub with a copy of *Manhunt* or *The Saint* and fall asleep. My mother would hear him snoring and go in too late to rescue a floating magazine.

I read what he read. I read what he didn't. One day I found a paperback in the back seat of the family car of a friend. It was a forbidden text with a provocative cover. It was Mickey Spillane's *My Gun Is Quick*. My friend's father said I could have it if my parents didn't object. Mick was pretty raw stuff back then. I assured my friend's father that my parents didn't care what I read. That was, in fact, true. And so I had the book. It proved to be as much fun as Oz.

I read it in one night. I began saving nickels and dimes, gathering bottles from alleys so I could return them for deposit money. I needed every penny I could gather so I could go to the movies, and to buy detective novels. My second paperback was *The Killer Inside Me* by Jim Thompson, chosen solely because of the cover art and title. This was definitely something I had to hide from my parents.

Back up a year or two. I did go to the library. I read randomly anything that seemed to be about something thrilling or scary. I read Nathaniel Hawthorne, Robert Louis Stevenson, Charles Dickens, and John Steinbeck. I was highly literate; I just didn't know it. But the library did not have Mickey Spillane or any Gold Medal books, or anything much that looked or read like a thin map-back. Such books, I discovered, were not considered "literature."

I hate the word "literature." It suggests a qualitative difference between the books and movies I loved and something "better." I was introduced to the concept of literature in school only after I had read *Ivanhoe, Treasure Island, Oliver Twist, Alice in Wonderland, Huckleberry Finn,* and *The Scarlet Letter.* To me, Hawthorne, Melville, Twain, and Stevenson were writers whose stories I loved in the same way I loved Spillane, Thompson, Cornell Woolrich, Lionel White, or Shepard Rifkin. There was no "literature." There were only books I liked to read and think about and dream about. My attitude has not changed, though I went on to earn an M.A. in English Literature.

Toby Peters was born of this amalgam of eclectic fiction, particularly the movies and detective fiction. To honor the importance of his birth, I gave my new character the names of my two sons, Toby and Peter. Toby Peters will not be demeaned by being dismissed as trivia. The Toby Peters books, like the movies and novels that inspired him and his friends, are celebrations of the nostalgia I feel. In other words, they were and are a part of the history of my life. They are every bit as important to me and what I am as the war in Vietnam, Joseph McCarthy, or famine in China. I hope the same can be said for those who read the Toby Peters tales.

My Toby Peters books are a celebration of nostalgia. Nostalgia, I repeat, is not trivial or insignificant. It is the stuff dreams are made of, but it is much more. It is the stuff our lives are made of.

Dorothy goes down the Yellow Brick Road in search of a gray Kansas, which, MGM tells us, is what she really wants and needs. The "real world Dorothy" in the film has no choice. The film not only says that she must return to reality, it tells us that she wants to return. No, it is Oz Dorothy really needs—and I need. When we close a book or walk out of a theater, we return to the real, gray world as Dorothy did. We must return. We don't have to like it.

What we, or at least I, want is a return to the world created on the sound stages and back lots of RKO, Columbia, 20th Century Fox, Republic, Monogram, and MGM's Oz, where there may be the body of a midget laying on the yellow bricks. There may be a foul-mouthed little man bitterly denouncing us, but it is the journey that draws us, makes us realize that there is more to our lives than the gray we call "reality."

I don't know where you are going, but Toby Peters and I will always be packed lightly and ready to go in search of the Wizard. May he turn out to be not a little man behind a curtain, but a massive, wondrous creature with a booming voice who wants nothing to do with the world we too often mistake for the only reality.

In the 1940s Los Angeles where Toby Peters, Phil Pevsner, Mrs. Plautt, Gunther Wherthman, Sheldon Mick, and Jeremy Butler reside, Erroll Flynn, Bette Davis, Clark Gable, Mae West, and dozens of others live again and are free to be what I would like to have them be. They are free to live again in my imagination and, I hope, in yours.

Stuart M. Kaminsky
Sarasota, Florida